Best Wishes
for
Christmas. 1942.

From Mum & Dad.
To. Eric.

WITH MORGAN ON THE MAIN

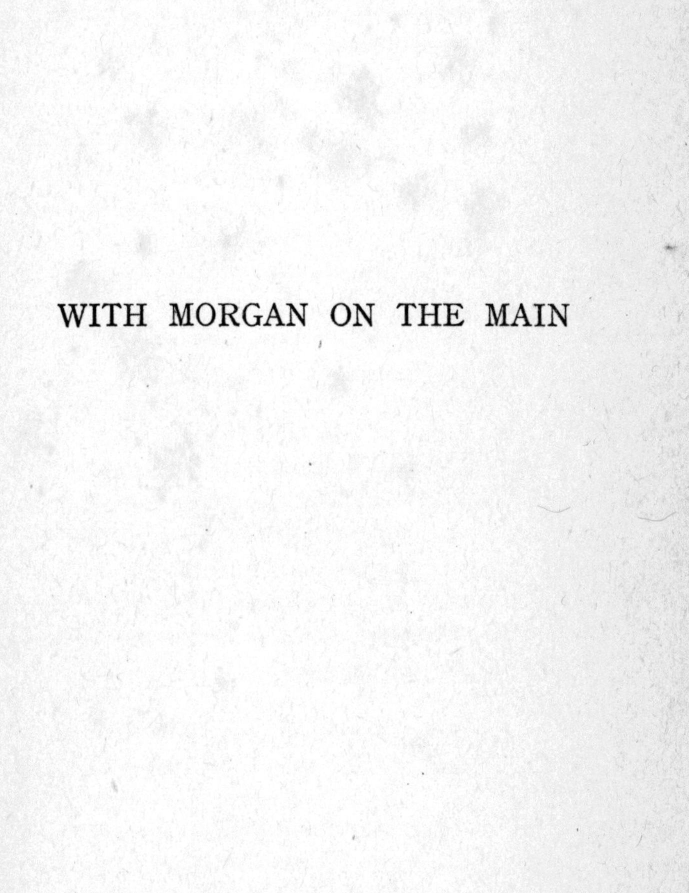

WE SOMETIMES HEARD MOVEMENTS OF THE CONCEALED SPANIARDS NEAR OUR ROUTE

WITH MORGAN ON THE MAIN

BY

C. M. BENNETT

DEAN & SON, LTD.

DEBRETT HOUSE, 41/43 LUDGATE HILL,

LONDON, E.C.4

MADE AND PRINTED IN GREAT BRITAIN

To

THE MASTERS AND BOYS

OF

CHESTERFIELD ROAD SCHOOL

Enfield

IN MEMORY OF THE HAPPY YEARS
SPENT WITH THEM

CONTENTS

CHAPTER		PAGE
I.	BESET BY GALLEONS . . .	11
II.	ABOARD THE "HELL-FIRE" . .	22
III.	MY MEETING WITH MORGAN .	38
IV.	MY FLIGHT FROM JAMAICA . .	50
V.	TROUBLE IN THE FLEET . .	64
VI.	NEWS OF MY FATHER . . .	76
VII.	THE SACK OF PORTO BELLO . .	89
VIII.	POLLY FLINDERS APPEARS . .	102
IX.	WE REACH MARACAYBO . .	118
X.	CAPTURED BY THE DONS . .	134
XI.	PEDRO THE HAIRY . . .	148
XII.	TRAPPED IN MARACAYBO LAGOON .	164
XIII.	THE WITCH OF PORT ROYAL .	179
XIV.	THE MARCH ACROSS THE ISTHMUS .	194
XV.	THE BATTLE BEFORE PANAMA .	212
XVI.	HOW I ENTERED THE CITY . .	225
XVII.	THE FALL OF PANAMA . . .	238

REWARD SERIES

THE REPUTATION OF THE UPPER FOURTH
CAPTAIN CAIN
THE PIRATE SUBMARINE
WITH MORGAN ON THE MAIN
THE FLYING SUBMARINE
A BUCCANEER'S LOG
MUTINY ISLAND
THE HONOUR OF THE SCHOOL
GUIDE GILLY
TIM KANE'S TREASURE
A YOUNG PRETENDER
A FIGHT FOR FORTUNE

CHAPTER I

BESET BY GALLEONS

As daily we drew nearer to Jamaica, where my father, Sir Hugh Ellis, had been appointed second in command, everybody aboard became anxious. It is true that our ship, the *Rover*, was well manned and armed, but the times were perilous, and Spanish galleons all too numerous in those waters.

"The Spaniards are not so daring as they were," Captain Barret informed my father, one day, as together they paced the quarter-deck. "The buccaneers are speedily driving them off the sea."

My father frowned. "I've heard of these buccaneers," said he. "Cattlemen turned sailors, aren't they? It seems a pity to me that the English Navy has to call upon the aid of such."

"Nay, Sir Hugh, you do the buccaneers scant justice. True it is that until a few months agone they looked after their cattle, and led a fairly peaceable life selling smoked meat to passing ships. The Spaniards themselves put an end to their trade by rounding up and killing the cattle which the buccaneers used to hunt. Whereupon the buccaneers took to the sea in Indian canoes, and whenever they caught sight of a Spanish ship pursued it, scrambled aboard, and more often than not, captured it. In this way they have built up quite a strong fleet, and have proved themselves clever sailors and daring fighters."

My father hummed a little tune, as though he hardly believed what Captain Barrett had said, whereupon the latter continued warmly:

"You still think, because they were once cattlemen, these buccaneers can't make good sailors. You will find your mistake, sir, in a very short time after landing at Jamaica. The Governor-General is working hard to keep them as a branch of the English Fleet."

The conversation was interrupted by a hail from the mast-head of "Sail in sight." Captain Barrett immediately called for its bearing, and then clapped his spy-glass to his eye, through which he scanned the distant horizon. When at last he turned again to my father, his face had taken on a serious expression.

"It's not one sail, Sir Hugh, but three," he said. "If they're Spaniards, as I suspect, let us hope we give them the slip. Three to one is long odds, and I'd rather not risk my ship in such a case."

He gave curt orders for further sail to be set, and altered our course by a few points. The *Rover* was pretty fast before a stiff breeze, and the men generally had little fear of being overtaken. Probably we should have escaped easily enough, had not two other ships appeared over the sky-line ahead, which meant that if these were foes, we were surrounded.

Captain Barrett bit his lower lip till the blood appeared. "I trust I am no coward," said he, "but any man might hesitate at odds of five to one."

"Tut, man, never lose heart," replied my father cheerily. "Men have faced longer odds and come safely through. Keep the *Rover* straight ahead, and we may be able to dispose of the enemy ships in front of us before those astern are within gun-shot."

This being of a certainty the wisest plan, Captain Barrett followed it, at the same time expressing the hope that the ships ahead might prove to be friends. Long before we were within range of the two vessels, however, the golden flag of Spain was seen through our spy-glasses to be flaunting from the mast-head of each vessel. Our decks had already been cleared for action, and now that he knew for certain how things stood, Captain Barrett proved himself the brave and efficient skipper we had heard him to be.

"We've long odds to fight against, lads," he cried to his men, whom he had ordered to be called together in the waist of the ship, "but never forget we're not beaten till the ship goes down under our feet. Ever heard of Sir Richard Grenville? Ah! I see by the way your eyes light up and your muscles stiffen, that you catch my meaning. Say, do you think we can win through?"

The confident cheers and shouts of "Ay, ay, siir! That we can and will!" that greeted the skipper's little speech filled me with assurance. Boy-like, I thought these brown-skinned, reckless, devil-may-care seamen quite invincible. It did not strike me that the seamen aboard the Spanish vessels might be every whit as brave. With practically no fear, but a great deal of eager curiosity, I stationed myself in the bow, determined to enjoy to the full my first sea-fight.

The men had by now returned to their stations, and with grim but eager faces were waiting for the enemy ships to come within range. Each gun's crew stood grouped about its piece, ready to trail it left or right according to the gunner's order.

The captain of each gun stood with lighted linstock, waiting the command to fire.

"D'you think you can reach them yet?" asked Captain Barrett of the master-gunner, a man who rejoiced in the nickname of "Swampy." As if in mockery at his question, the nearer of the Spanish ships ahead fired a round which dropped close enough for its splash to wet me, and made my father curtly order me to get under cover.

"What the Don can do, we can, sir," quoth Swampy, sighting his gun; and receiving permission from the skipper, he applied the linstock and stood erect to watch the effect of his shot.

"Hurrah!" he cried, and flung his hat in the air, while the men who could see joined in his jubilation. His shot had fallen upon the deck of the foremost Spaniard, and the men seemed to consider this first success as a happy omen for a victorious issue.

As our own vessel and the two ahead rapidly approached, the guns on both sides were worked as hard as they could be loaded, laid, and fired. Very soon the Spaniard's balls were dropping aboard us, and I discovered for the first time that there was an ugly side to a sea-fight, very different from the heroic picture my young imagination had painted. Long before the vessels had approached near enough for boarding to be considered, our casualties had become so numerous that the surgeon and his few unskilled helpers had far more work than they could cope with. It is a hard thing to see men struck down by flying splinters, to see huge gashes cut, even limbs lopped off, without an enemy appearing within weapon's length. I grew sick at the sight of mangled bodies on the deck, and would have rushed away below, had it not been for my father's quiet suggestion that I should help in dressing wounds.

Subduing my fear as best I could, I followed him on his round of mercy, and with his calm, resolute bearing to strengthen me, feel sure that I did not disgrace myself. Indeed, after a time, so much was there to be done that I almost became oblivious of the dangers surrounding us, and of the rush and scurry of the men as powder and shot were carried up from below. Looking up on one occasion from a seaman whose leg had been carried away, I was surprised to find the tall spars of one of the Spanish ships towering above us, and next moment I heard the stentorian voice of Captain Barrett yelling out to his crew, "Prepare to repel boarders!" Forgetting the task in hand, I jumped to my feet, rushed to the racks where pikes and cutlasses were hung, and, seizing one of the former, hastened to the side where danger threatened.

The first grappling-hooks flung from the Spaniard's deck had been dislodged, but more now fell aboard us, and such a raking volley of musket shot swept our decks that it would have been madness to have tried to fling them off. We had, perforce, to crouch under cover of the bulwarks till the musket-fire should slacken, and the enemy come swarming up our sides.

As the two ships gradually drew together, Captain Barrett, noticing the despondent looks of some of his men, shouted out to know where Fiddler Jim was. The man called for crawled out from cover, his beloved fiddle slung, as usual, across his shoulders.

"Give us one of your capstan-bar tunes, my lad!" cried the skipper, and Fiddler Jim's eyes glistened at the chance. Little did he reck of musket-ball or arrow as he unslung his instrument, tucked it jauntily under his chin, and drew his bow across the strings. Merrily his fingers moved, and quickly rose and fell his bow arm as the gladsome strains of an Irish jig sounded eerily above the noise of the battle. The big guns had practically ceased their fire, but of noise there was plenty. Cutlasses clashed, whistles blew, muskets cracked, and the roar of orders sounded above the hum of the men about to meet in dreadful combat. Yet over all the din could be heard the strains of the fiddle as Jim strutted up and down the deck, sending a message of encouragement to our men.

"Now then, lads. Don't give way an inch!" shouted a voice near by, and I knew the boarding party was upon us. Up scrambled the Spaniards, like so many wild cats, some bearing their weapons in their mouths, others, armed with axes, striking these deep into the *Rover's* side, to help themselves upwards. Our men below decks stabbed at the boarders through the port-holes, sending many headlong into the sea. On came the rest, heedless of their comrades' fate, and manfully we met them, determined not to let them make good footing upon our decks.

One I stabbed with the long pike I had seized, and back he fell with a loud scream, suddenly cut short as the waves closed over his head. I tried to treat another in the same way, but he seized the pike, just above its point, and for some moments we contended for the weapon. Then it struck me that if I let go the pike, the Spaniard would fall into the sea, so I released my weapon, and watched the Don carry it with him down to the narrow stretch of water that separated the two vessels.

Curiosity to see the end of my antagonist was nearly my undoing. A swarthy Spaniard clutched me round the neck, and it seemed I must either allow myself to be dragged overboard, or be used as a lever for the Spaniard to hoist himself to our decks. Fiddler Jim settled the matter by lunging at my assailant with a pike, whereupon the fellow hurriedly let go, and fell back upon a comrade below.

There followed a few minutes of hard fighting which has left but hazy impressions in my memory. I have an idea that once I was borne down to the deck, and I believe it was my father who rescued me. Then I remember seeing the giant of the crew (Big Dixon he was called) carrying two of the foe, like a pair of kittens, each by the scruff of his neck to the ship's side, there to pitch them overboard. Also I remember seeing Fiddler Jim, instrument and all, dragged over the side, and carried away, still struggling with his opponent, by the foaming sea.

My next really clear recollection came when there ensued a lull in the fighting, and I realised the Spaniard was drawing away from us. The grappling irons had been dislodged, and the two vessels had yawed somewhat apart. A few of the Spaniards remained clinging to our sides, but most of them, seeing their danger, had leapt back to their own ship. Captain Barrett was just the man to grasp the situation, and he issued his orders crisply.

Himself he took the helm and kept the *Rover* on her original course By this manœuvre he had only to pass the second Spaniard to have all five foes astern, when, with a little luck, he might show them all a clean pair of heels. As we passed, she gave us a ragged broadside, but her shot did not cause much damage, probably because our escape from her sister ship had been unexpected. Anyway we sailed by, our sweating seamen giving her a derisive cheer as we passed, and as Captain Barrett cast his eyes astern, a satisfied smile lit up his face.

"It will take those two more than a minute to turn about in chase of us," he chuckled. "As for the three still farther astern, I think we have the heels of those. I believe we shall have luck enough to sail into a Jamaican harbour yet."

Like the skipper, the men were jubilant. They exchanged rough jests about their pursuers which were tacking about so as once again to come in chase of us. But one of the Spaniards was quickly turned, and Captain Barrett looked grave again as he found her in hot pursuit long before he had expected.

"Whoever commands that ship—Spaniard or no—is a fine sailor!" he declared, real admiration in his eyes. "All the same, I think we shall win clear."

And so we should have done, but for a lucky shot from the foremost Spaniard. We were almost out of range and preening ourselves upon our good fortune when the shot came, bringing down our main-mast, already heavily scarred in the earlier gun duel.

Two men were killed outright by the fall of the mast, half a dozen were injured. Those left, urged on by the skipper and his mates, made some attempt to cut away the wreckage, but their efforts were but half-hearted, as though they knew it was now impossible to escape.

My father held a hurried consultation with the skipper.

"You too!" I heard the latter say. "It is my duty to insist upon your taking whatever chance of escape may exist."

My father shook his head, smiling a little sadly the while.

"Don't think I want to fall into the hands of the Spaniards, any more than the rest of you," he said, "but don't expect me to shield myself behind the word 'duty' so that I can desert."

Captain Barrett still attempted to argue with my father, but was not allowed to proceed. "No, captain," said my father, in such definite tones as to prohibit any further discussion, "I'm staying here with the rest, come what may. If you and your men have to endure prison, perhaps even torture and death, I claim the right to share the same fate. But I shall thankfully accept your offer of a boat and a man to row it, to give my son a chance of getting away."

This was the first notion I had that my father purposed to enable me to escape the coming boarding. I could read his thoughts. A small boat, lowered at once, would probably escape the notice of the oncoming galleons in the heat of the battle, and even if seen, the Spaniards would hardly deem it worth their while to pursue. Captain Barrett showed me my surmise was correct by detailing men to lower the gig, and to see that it was well stored with water and provisions.

At that I flung myself at my father, hugging him fiercely, and begged him not to send me away. "I am no coward," I cried; "why make me one? Let me stay with you."

"My son," said my father gently, "it will not be

cowardice on your part to leave the *Rover*, since it is my wish. You have your life before you while we, who may soon be killed, have passed our prime."

But I begged him the harder to let me stay. It seemed too cowardly for any one, man or boy, to leave his shipmates to almost certain death or capture.

"Very well!" exclaimed my father at length. "Since my persuasions won't make you go, I'll order you. What man have you detailed to go with the boy, captain?"

"I can only spare one, Sir Hugh, as I told you, but I will give you the best I have aboard. Send Big Dixon to me, Mr. Adams," he added, turning to his first mate.

Big Dixon came, stripped to his waist, and shining with sweat, for none had fought harder than he, nor worked more strenuously to clear away the wreckage. He was a man of about thirty, six foot high, with massive shoulders. He was somewhat clumsy to look at, for his body was thick throughout, and he might even have been called slightly stout. Yet despite this, he was light and active in his movements, nor was there another man aboard who possessed his great strength.

Captain Barrett quickly explained to the man what he was to do. "If you can escape notice," he concluded, "make for the nearest land. Try to get a passage to Port Royal, and there deliver over the boy to the Governor-General, and tell him what has chanced to Sir Hugh Ellis and the rest of us. It is not necessary for me to tell you to guard this lad with your own life!"

Big Dixon was about to speak, as I believe to ask whether some one else might not be given this chance of escape while he stayed with his messmates, but before he could do so, my father had stepped forward, and seized him by the hand.

"I know you are fond of my boy, Dixon," he said, "and I know I can trust you to do your utmost to carry him to safety. God bless you!"

Tears stood in the honest fellow's eyes.

"I will do my best, Sir Hugh, and no man can say more," he said simply, "but this I can swear. If any ill chance does happen to your lad, it will not be through any fault of mine. And till he finds you again, or returns in safety to England, I promise you I'll follow him wherever he may go."

CHAPTER II

ABOARD THE "HELL-FIRE"

ALL the time the gig was being lowered and provisioned, the enemy guns—nor ours neither, for that matter—had not been idle. When Big Dixon actually pushed off from the *Rover's* side, the foremost of our pursuers could have been little more than two hundred yards astern, and coming up hand over hand.

The sea was far from calm, and there was a big possibility of our cockleshell of a boat being overwhelmed by the great waves that now tossed us up like a cork upon their crests, now flung us down into a vale as though meaning to engulf us. Fortunately Big Dixon was a skilful oarsman, keeping the boat as well as he could before the wind, so that we shipped little water. For myself I was so desperately downhearted at having had to leave my father to death or captivity that the danger of drowning worried me not a jot. Perhaps the heavy sea that was running was the means of our escaping unseen, for apart from one shot that fell unpleasantly close just after we left the *Rover's* side, no further notice whatever was taken of us.

Big Dixon, seeing my downcast looks, presently found the means to occupy my thoughts. In a kindly voice he bade me see to the baling of the boat. "Keep your pecker up, lad," he added. "Your father is more likely to be taken prisoner than killed, and how will you be able to rescue him if you let yourself be drowned?"

Here was a new thought that served to rouse me. If indeed my father were taken prisoner by the Spaniards, all the time I was free there might be a chance to rescue him. Therefore with a will I set to work to rid the boat of the water which had slopped aboard, and for some five minutes was so busily engaged as almost to forget my peril.

When next I caught a glimpse of the *Rover*, I found she was sandwiched between two of the Spanish galleons, and over the waves came the din of the boarders as they dashed upon the depleted English crew. The noise of the conflict did not last long. As I looked I had the mortification of seeing the English flag hauled down, and in its place were run up the colours of Spain.

Big Dixon, who had watched this procedure with a scowl, dug his sculls fiercely into the water, as though to give vent to his hurt feelings. But before he had made a dozen more strokes, I heard a faint hail from our left, and looking in that direction, espied a swimmer feebly splashing on the crest of a wave.

"Quick, Dick," I shouted (for Big Dixon's name was usually shortened to Dick when anyone addressed him); "quick! There's a swimmer yonder."

Big Dixon made no answer in words, but he swung the boat round in the direction in which I pointed, and presently we were hauling a damp, helpless figure over the stern.

It is a wonder we were not swamped in the proceeding, for the swimmer could do nothing to help himself. Somehow or other we managed it, Big Dixon leaning over and hauling up the drowning man, while I did all I could to steady the boat. Presently the man was laid, face downwards, in the bottom, whereupon Big Dixon and I had to bale like men possessed to free the boat of the water she had shipped.

"Why, surely it's Fiddler Jim!" I exclaimed, when we were able to rest from our labours. "See, he still has his fiddle strapped to his shoulders. He'll not be able to play it again, though, I'll be bound. It's suffered more from its ducking than he has."

"He'll be all right soon enough," agreed Big Dixon, "but he'll be sore downhearted when he sees what has happened to his fiddle. He loves that instrument better than many a man loves his firstborn."

We could do but little to aid Fiddler Jim's recovery. Big Dixon was anxious to carry out the wishes of my father by taking me safely to land, and as his first business was to put as great a distance as he could between ourselves and the Spanish galleons, he bent sturdily at the sculls. My task of baling the boat could not be left for more than a few minutes at a time, or we should have foundered. Therefore, apart from arranging Fiddler Jim so that any water he had swallowed might trickle from his mouth, we left him to recover as best he could.

Presently he groaned, and then he gave vent to an oath. After a while he began to swing his arms about, as though still swimming for his life; and finally, with a sudden heave, he sat himself up in the boat and unslung the fiddle from his shoulders.

"Ah, ruined, ruined," he chanted miserably, apparently forgetting how near he himself had been to death, so that by comparison the loss of his instrument was but an unimportant affair. Big Dixon tried to point this out to him, but the little man would have none of it, and continued his lamentations.

"Where shall I find such another instrument?" said he. "My father used it, and his father before him. I have carried it with me for twenty years, ashore and afloat. How shall I get along without it?"

"Best wait till we are on dry land again, Jim," I suggested. "That will be time enough to worry about your fiddle. Maybe it can be mended, but so far as I can see you're not likely to need to play it again, save possibly to Father Neptune at the bottom of the sea."

"Stow that talk," bade Big Dixon. "We'll not drown this trip, I'll wager. As for you, Fiddler, quit weeping over your fiddle, and give the boy a hand with his baling."

But not until he had emptied his instrument of salt-water, and placed it as safely as he could on one of the seats of the boat, tied thereto with his neckerchief to save it from being washed away, would the fiddler do as he was told. Even when he did take the tin from my hand, and commence the ever-necessary task of keeping the boat free from water, every now and again he would look at his beloved fiddle with such sorrow in his eyes that I could not help feeling sympathy.

By nightfall the Spanish galleons, with the *Rover* to keep them company, had vanished over the sky-line, and I cannot tell how despondent I felt as they sailed away. My father and I had always been firm friends, and of a sudden I had found myself, with two others, in an open boat upon a ruffled sea, uncertain whether he was still alive. Even if he had not been killed, he was a prisoner in Spanish hands, and it was all too common knowledge how brutally they treated English seamen who fell into their power.

It was fortunate, on the whole, that my own perilous position kept me from thinking too much of my father's fate. All through the night we pitched and tossed upon the restless sea, unable to sleep, cold and tired, yet forced continually to bale the boat free from water. Dawn found us alone in the midst of the sea. We scanned the ocean around, yet no sign of land nor vessel met our anxious gaze. We continued our labours to keep afloat, while the sun mounted higher and higher in the sky, till it stood almost directly overhead, and its heat was well-nigh unbearable. Our misery was somewhat alleviated by the sea becoming calmer, which gave us the opportunity to rest from our labours, and take a much-needed meal. But the heat was too fierce by far for us to sleep, and we lay gasping at the bottom of the boat, praying for night and its coolness.

Big Dixon arranged that we should watch in turns during the night. He himself was to take the first watch, Jim the second, and myself the last. Later I learned that Dixon had kept awake, despite his fatigue, for more than half the night, and had then called upon Fiddler Jim to relieve him. The Fiddler did his best to keep awake while I lay curled up in the bows, and Big Dixon snored lustily in the stern. However, the solitude proved too much for him. That, combined with the sufferings he had endured, and the gentle rocking of the boat on the now calmly swelling sea, lulled him to sleep again. Thus it was that we had no warning of the coming of the *Hell-Fire* till it loomed black above us in the first rays of the rising sun.

Big Dixon was the first to wake, and his shout of alarm aroused Jim and myself. We woke to see, as I have said, a sinister-looking ship towering above us. Looking down at us we could see a half-dozen faces that our surprise made appear even more ugly and terrible than they really were.

"We'll drop you a rope," came a voice from above. "Wait a minute."

We could do nothing else, and when presently the rope was lowered, Big Dixon set us an example by clambering aboard. I followed close behind him, and Jim came last, first taking care, however, to bring his beloved violin, damaged though it was, bound to his shoulders.

On deck we found ourselves confronted by seven or eight villainous-looking fellows, who kept us covered with their muskets.

"There's no need to be afraid of us," expostulated Big Dixon. "We're unarmed, and there are only three of us."

One of the fellows gave a rough chuckle. "Don't think we're afraid of you," said he, "but we believe in taking no risks. D'you know how many of us first captured this vessel? Six of us, in an open boat, and she carried a full muster of Spaniards aboard! All the same I don't think we've anything to fear from you. Put away your weapons, all but Red Pete, and haul up that boat. You fellows come along with me. Keep your eye on them, Pete, and see that they get up to no tricks."

We obeyed the man's orders, for obviously he had some sort of position aboard, nor would it have served any good purpose to refuse. The man's manner was not unfriendly, and at first I believed we had been picked up by an English trading-vessel. Big Dixon enlightened me as to the true character of the men into whose hands we had fallen by the single whispered word, "Buccaneers," as we were led below.

Buccaneers! I recalled in an instant the conversation I had heard between my father and Captain Barrett aboard the *Rover*. "Cattlemen turned sailors" had been my father's contemptuous description of them, but Captain Barrett had given them a much better report. I remembered that he had said the buccaneers were acting as a part of the English Navy, in which case we should probably be glad that our fate had led us to be picked up by one of their ships.

Our guide led us to a barely-furnished cabin, where he bade us be seated. He then asked how we had come to be adrift in an open boat, and Big Dixon gave him the required information as clearly and directly as he could.

While Dixon was speaking, I took stock of the buccaneer. He was a tall lean man, clad simply in rough clothes that left his hairy chest, long arms and legs, quite naked. These were tanned dark-brown by constant exposure to sun and air, as was also his face. His features were regular, if somewhat large. His eyes were dark and fierce-looking, his eyebrows heavily marked, his hair jet-black and matted. What struck me most of all about him was his fearless bearing and the general air of grim resolution that marked him out as a man that no difficulties would overawe.

He appeared quite satisfied with Big Dixon's tale, but said he would have to report our rescue to his captain, who had not yet risen. Till he made his report we were to remain in the cabin, whither he would presently send food and dry clothes. With this promise he and Red Pete both left us, locking the cabin door as they went out.

Big Dixon and I sat in silence after the buccaneer had left us. As for Fiddler Jim, he took advantage of being aboard again to examine his violin. I was amazed at the gentle way he fingered it all over, first wiping it carefully with a piece of cloth he found in the cabin. Truly, as Big Dixon had said, he loved his instrument better than many a man loved his first-born. I, for one, shared in his joy when presently, with a smile that lit up his whole face, he announced that the instrument was not utterly spoilt.

"It will never be quite the same again, though," he said, not quite so joyously. "Yet it will last me for the rest of my life if it gets no more bad treatment. How I wish I had my bow here, so that it could speak to me again," and he twanged the strings lovingly with his fingers.

The buccaneer was as good as his word, for we had not long to wait for dry clothes and a hot meal. As Big Dixon remarked, somewhat inaudibly since his great mouth was full and working strenuously as he spoke, it appeared that to fall into the hands of the buccaneers was far better than falling into the power of the Dons.

I was not so sure about it when we were led, some two hours later, into the presence of the skipper of the buccaneer ship. Many of the crew stood about, and I had never before clapped eyes upon a more savage-looking lot of men. The skipper himself was a tall, fleshy man, tremendous in bulk, and obviously powerful. He was dressed in much the same fashion as his men—loose trousers reaching half-way down his bare legs, coloured shirt open at the neck, while round his prominent paunch was strapped a belt into which were stuck a brace of pistols and a long, keen knife. Though his face could hardly be described as pleasant-looking, partly owing to its flabbiness, and partly to an ugly, crooked scar, yet there was nothing particularly ferocious about it, and I regained something of the assurance of safety which the villainous looks of his crew had taken from me.

"Well, my hearties!" he exclaimed, after a long scrutiny. "My mate, Harvey, has told me you have escaped from a Spanish attack. Best tell me your tale again, so that I get it right."

Big Dixon did so, and then the buccaneer skipper, who rejoiced in the inappropriate name of Captain Gentle, asked us questions in turn. Our answers soon convinced him that our story was true, and when he learned who my father was, he treated me with a respect which reminded me that the buccaneers were largely under the control of the Governor-General of Jamaica. He seemed chiefly interested in learning in which direction the Spaniards had sailed with their prize, and then, after some consideration, he announced that the course of the *Hell-Fire* was to be set direct for Jamaica.

"These Spanish dogs are getting too venturesome," he asserted. "Perhaps they'll keep their galleons off the high seas when the walls of Porto Bello begin to tumble about their ears."

"D'you mean we're going to sack——" began Harvey the mate.

"Never you mind what I mean," replied Captain Gentle, with a pronounced wink. "But remember the Dons think Porto Bello can't be taken, and we Brethren of the Coast believe there's no place that can't be taken if you've men brave enough to tackle the job. We'll see whether the Dons or the buccaneers are right all in good time."

With a warning to his crew not to molest me, Captain Gentle lumbered away, leaving the rest of us to be surrounded by the *Hell-Fire's* crew.

Evidently Captain Gentle knew it was the custom for newcomers falling into the buccaneers' hands to be subjected to numerous petty tyrannies, hence his warning to his men concerning myself, which saved me from annoyance. Big Dixon and Fiddler Jim were not so fortunate, and the buccaneers set themselves the task of finding out what sort of stuff my messmates were made of.

Big Dixon, doubtless owing to his size, was the first butt of their remarks and acts. Rude remarks anent his size Dixon took with a stupid-looking grin though I caught a gleam in his eyes that told me his tormentors would do well not to overstep a certain limit. Finding their verbal jests having apparently no effect, the buccaneers proceeded to acts, prodding him as though he were a prize pig being inspected and pinching and thumping him as though he had no feelings. Big Dixon stuck it for a time, probably thinking it best not to anger the buccaneers if it could be avoided. His patience evaporated, however, when two of the ruffians started prodding him with their keen-pointed knives. With the bellow of a wounded bull, Dixon sprang at his tormentors, seized one in either hand by the scruff of the neck, and brought their heads together with a resounding smack.

One fell at once to the deck like a pole-axed bull. The other swayed dizzily about till he managed to cling hold of a rope for support, where he stood stupidly, trying to steady himself, and wondering, no doubt, whether or no his head was cracked. As for the remaining buccaneers, they were delighted with what had befallen their comrades, and ceased to worry Big Dixon with their witticisms, which were directed, instead, against the dazed sufferer from Dixon's attack.

This latter I recognised as our acquaintance of the morning, Red Pete, his nickname being doubtless bestowed because of his mass of flaming red hair. It took him quite a while to recover, long enough for a bucket of water to be dashed over his more unfortunate comrade, who was roughly carried to his bunk directly this rude treatment had brought him back to partial consciousness. When Red Pete did eventually stand steady again, there was a ferocious look upon his face which boded ill to Big Dixon.

"You swab!" he said thickly, between clenched teeth. "I believe you've cracked my skull."

This dolorous statement was greeted with roars of laughter and chaff from his comrades, which served still further to increase Red Pete's wrath.

"And now I'm going to slit your windpipe," he cried, and next moment an ugly knife flashed in his hand.

"Am I not to have a weapon?" demanded Big Dixon, stepping backwards. Before answer could be made, or weapon proffered, Red Pete was upon him, knife uplifted ready to strike.

The attack was so sudden and so ferocious that it was a wonder Big Dixon was not struck down.

Once the knife descended, and when it rose again, to my horror it was dull with blood. Before it could again descend Big Dixon's upflung hand had closed about his antagonist's wrist.

There followed a short trial of strength; but though wounded, Big Dixon was far too powerful for Red Pete. Back, back, back he pressed the buccaneer's knife-arm, until Red Pete's hand opened, and the knife clattered harmlessly to the deck. Still Big Dixon did not cease his pressure. Back he pressed Red Pete's arm, till the buccaneer's face was twisted with pain. There came a sudden snap, just as a twig will crack beneath one's foot in a wood. Then only did Big Dixon cease his pressure, whereupon Red Pete's broken arm fell limply to his side.

Big Dixon did not stand long to enjoy his triumph. Already a big patch of blood had stained the front of his shirt. He tottered, and made a desperate effort to keep his balance. It was too much for him. His knees sagged, and he fell, unconscious.

I was beside him in a trice, half-crazed with fear. Partly I was terrified for my own sake, for if Big Dixon died, I knew I had lost a powerful protector. To my boy's eyes he possessed all the qualities of a first-class hero, and I dreaded lest this man whom I loved should die.

Ripping open his shirt, I found an ugly, gaping wound in his left shoulder. Before I could do aught to stop the bleeding, Harvey, the mate, had pushed me roughly aside.

"I'll soon patch this fellow up," said he. "He's too good a fighter to lose, so we'll doctor him, and then I'll have him carried below to my own bunk."

The mate was as good as his word. As I saw the skilful way he bound my messmate's wound, my fears for Dick's safety disappeared. Though he did not recover consciousness before he was carried below, I knew, without Harvey's assurance, that there was no danger. In fact, the buccaneer told me that my friend (or, as he said, my *matelot*) would be fit and about again in less than a week.

Fiddler Jim had been a quiet spectator of all that had transpired. It was now his turn to be tormented. Red Pete's broken arm was roughly put into splints, and then all the buccaneers not actually injured or working the ship gathered round the luckless Jim.

One of them laid his hand upon the precious fiddle, whereupon Jim jumped to his feet with an oath, and dared the man to touch his violin again.

His defiance was greeted with rough cheers and mock applause. "Give us a tune on your old fiddle," cried one. "Yes," agreed another, "and if your music don't please us we'll break your fiddle over your head."

Fiddler Jim's face went white. As he told me afterwards, how could he know how his violin would play after the rough usage it had received.

"I've no bow," he cried, "and one of the strings is broken. Can't you see——"

"Where's poor old Bill Lorrimore's fiddle?" asked Harvey. "When he got knocked out, who got his fiddle?"

"I did, mates. It's down below, and I'll fetch it up in a jiffy." The short, slim man who had spoken slipped away below, and presently returned with a broken fiddle, and a bow.

"I sat on the fiddle the other night," said the little man, in explanation of the violin's condition, "but the strings are all right. So is the bow."

"Hand 'em over to this fiddler," commanded Harvey. "Now, my lad," he continued, to Fiddler Jim, "you've got the instrument that used to belong to the best scraper in the buccaneer fleet. He'd be here playing to us to-day, only he stopped a musket-ball a fortnight back. Hurry up and put your fiddle in order, so that we can hear if you're worthy of taking Bill Lorrimore's place."

Seeing there was no help for it, Fiddler Jim used one of the strings from the broken violin to replace the damaged one of his own instrument. Actually I think the chance of playing again delighted him, except for the threat of having his fiddle broken if his performance did not satisfy his rough audience.

"Cut out the frills," shouted one of the buccaneers as Jim began to tune his fiddle, and others joined in the cry. Unperturbed, Jim continued his tuning. "How d'you expect me to play with a violin out of tune?" he demanded angrily, as the buccaneers continued to shout at him.

At length he was ready. One of the men lifted him bodily, and set him astride the breech of one of the guns. The rest stood or sat expectantly around.

Fiddler Jim tucked his violin under his chin, and poised his bow uncertainly over the strings, as though undecided what to play. Then, with a quick flourish he had started. His fingers danced merrily from string to string, his bow moved to and fro in lightning passes, as once again he played the merry Irish Jig which had so heartened the men of the *Rover* when the Spaniards had been on the point of boarding her.

It was too much for the buccaneers. How could they talk of breaking the fiddle of a man who could play like this? Their feet began to mark time to the music, their bodies swayed to the lilt of it. Presently Harvey seized me by the waist and began to dance with me to and fro, and round about, till my head grew dizzy. His example was followed by most of his comrades, and very soon Fiddler Jim was surrounded by a score of clumsily-dancing couples, while most of the buccaneers added to the general hilarity by joining their raucous voices to swell the music of the violin.

The dance was at its height when Captain Gentle appeared. He stood at first, arms akimbo, watching the antics of his men, but when one of them, quitting his partner, flung his arms around the skipper, crying upon him to join in, he did so with an energy that scattered other dancers before him like autumn leaves before a hurricane, while his great voice boomed out (as he fondly imagined) in tune with the fiddle.

When the men had tired of dancing, and lay, gasping for breath, about the deck, Fiddler Jim ceased his playing, but there came an immediate demand for more. So Jim gave them what I should have been afraid to have presented to such a gang of ruffians, a haunting melody that brought tears to my eyes. The buccaneers ceased their clamour, and listened in awed silence as the beautiful notes were drawn out by the bow.

"Fetch up some rum, Harvey!" quoth Captain Gentle, when the tune was finished. "This is an occasion for a toast." And when each man was served, he stood over by Fiddler Jim, with cup uplifted.

"Brethren of the Coast," he said, "drink to our new comrade, Fiddler Jim. Here and now we appoint him Fiddler-in-Chief to the whole buccaneer fleet."

Amid loud huzzas the toast was drunk.

CHAPTER III

MY MEETING WITH MORGAN

Two days later, when I came on deck, I found the *Hell-Fire* had run during night into harbour. Seven other big ships swung there at anchor, and at the mast-head of each fluttered a flag bearing a red cross upon a white background.

I asked Harvey, who stood near me, the name of the port, though I could have made a pretty shrewd guess that it was Port Royal, the chief town of Jamaica, where my father was to have taken up his duties. I could not help thinking of my loss as I stood looking across at the white building which I guessed to be the Governor-General's residence, and which, so I dolefully told myself, my father would never live to enter. Resolutely, however, I flung off this fit of sadness. I had made up my mind what to do. Somehow or other I would find out what had been my father's fate aboard the *Rover*, and if he had been taken prisoner—as I hardly dared to hope—I would seek out his prison and do my utmost to release him.

Harvey, who was in a talkative mood, told me that the flags flying at the mast-heads of the ships at anchor were of a design chosen by the Confederacy of the Buccaneers. "At present our fleet is working alongside the English Navy," he explained, "but how long we shall do so is another thing. Many of the Brethren of the Coast want to seize one of the islands hereabouts, and set up a state of our own."

"Who would you make chief of your state?" I asked.

"That's a big question. The Dutch would like Mansvelt, and I'm not saying he isn't a good man. But you mark my words, there's a Welshman who'll very soon be Admiral of the Buccaneer Fleet or I'm a parson. Then let the Spaniards beware!"

"I've heard that the Spanish galleons are already avoiding these waters," said I, "though perhaps that is untrue. There were five of them in sight the day we lost our ship."

"There are few enough, Arthur, you may be sure of that. And those that remain rarely sail alone; in fact, more often than not they lie at anchor under the guns of Spanish strongholds."

"Then how is this Welshman—you did not say his name—going to injure the Spaniards?" I asked.

"How?" responded Harvey. "Why, he'll not worry about the Spanish galleons at all. He'll attack and sack the Spanish strongholds themselves, where they store up the jewels and gold they've stolen from the Incas' mines. It is already freely whispered that Morgan—that's the Welshman's name, mark it well! —that Morgan intends taking Porto Bello. If he's successful, there's some that say he'll be ready to lead us across the Isthmus itself, to Golden Panama!"

As Harvey spoke, he flung out his chest and his fists clenched tightly. Ruffian he might be, but he was more than that. He was an adventurer, and the thought of taking part in daring exploits thrilled him far more than any hopes of booty to be gained in consequence.

It was high noon before Captain Gentle came on deck prepared to pay a visit ashore. He had already ordered Big Dixon and myself to be ready to accompany him, and we had waited impatiently for over an hour for his appearance. Dixon's wound was by now well on the way to recovery, and he was in high spirits at the thought of being able to keep his promise to my father by handing me safely over to the Governor-General of Jamaica.

The journey up to the Governor-General's residence was full of interest. We passed along mean, often dirty streets, and it amazed me to note the great number of rum-shops, each of which appeared to have enough customers to fill it. More than ever it became apparent to me how big a position the buccaneers had now taken in the affairs of these islands. There were scores of them ashore, drinking or lounging about, and their bronzed skins and general air of reckless courage gave them all a formidable appearance.

We were kept waiting for upwards of an hour at the Governor-General's, and one of the soldiers in attendance whispered to us that Harry Morgan had been in conference with the Governor since nine o'clock that morning. But Captain Gentle was not one to be kept kicking his heels in an ante-room, whether for Governor-General or Admiral of the Buccaneers. After waiting a longer time than I expected him to, during which he growled and snarled like a dog deprived of its bone, he sent in a curt message that "Captain Gentle of the *Hell-Fire*, together with young Master Arthur Ellis, son of Sir Hugh Ellis (whom perhaps the Governor had heard of), had waited for an hour for an audience, and would wait five more minutes." Either the audacity of the message, or the mention of my father's name, brought an immediate response. We were ushered straightway into the presence of the two chief men of the Island.

The Governor-General was a short, white-haired, insignificant-looking man, and I did not spend much time in looking at him. It was Morgan who claimed my chief attention. Seated as he was at the polished table, I could not judge his full height, but guessed it was at any rate above the average. His shoulders were broad and square, his neck thick, and his jaw jutted out in a most formidable manner. What struck me most of all were his eyes—black, flashing ones, that seemed to look right through you, and read your inmost thoughts. Seeing me looking at him so fixedly, the Admiral turned his piercing eyes upon me, and chuckled to himself when, unable to meet his fierce gaze, I looked instead at the toes of my shoes.

My attention was recalled to the Governor-General by a question from him in his quiet, gentle voice, asking for news of my father. When I told him what had happened, his face grew grave, and I noticed that his long slender hands trembled. "This is indeed sad news," he said, as I finished my tale. "Your father and I are old friends. I sincerely trust he was taken prisoner and not killed when the *Rover* was captured."

"Better to die than to be a prisoner in the hands of the Dons," interrupted Morgan in a rough voice, and I knew he was right. I had seen Englishmen who had escaped from Spanish hands, most of them so enfeebled by privations and ofttimes torture, that life was a burden to them.

"Perhaps you are right, Admiral," agreed the Governor courteously, "but while life remains there is hope. We must try to find out from our spies what has happened to Sir Hugh Ellis. If he is a prisoner, we must do our utmost to ransom him."

"Or batter down his prison walls to release him," cried Morgan. "If I and my buccaneers knew where he was imprisoned, we would free him, if it meant crossing the Isthmus to do it."

How my heart warmed to Morgan as he uttered this speech. I felt confident that if my father lived Morgan and his buccaneers would release him. In that moment was born a resolve to attach myself, somehow or other, to Morgan's crew, so that if once I could find out in what prison my father was held (I would not admit to myself the possibility of him being dead), I could remind the Admiral of his promise to free him.

It is one thing to resolve, another to carry out a resolution. I found that when my future came up for discussion, the Governor had very different views. Timidly I expressed my wish to join the ranks of the buccaneers. Morgan, with an oath, clapped me on the back and told me I was "a bold blade." Captain Gentle showed his appreciation by a loud huzza, which he attempted, with indifferent success, to turn into a cough. The Governor was very quiet, but determined. "It's no place for a boy upon a buccaneer's ship," said he. "You shall take up your residence with me. I will engage a tutor to look after you, and in due course, if no news comes to hand concerning your father, I will arrange for you to be taken back to England."

I attempted to argue, but he speedily cut me short. Insignificant he might look, but he possessed a will too strong for me openly to oppose.

Permission was given me to return to Captain Gentle's ship, there to say farewell to Fiddler Jim and other friends I had made. Big Dixon was given orders to accompany me, for the streets of Port Royal were not always safe in those rough days. As we threaded our way back to the *Hell-fire* I noticed my companion seemed very down-hearted, and asked him the cause.

"You remember what I said to your father about keeping with you?" he said. "I've kept my promise up to a point, but I want to do more. You've got to go to the Governor's to live, and I shall get a berth aboard some ship. What I hoped to do was to join you in finding your father."

I gripped him warmly by the hand.

"So you shall," I cried, and I told him my plan. Straightway he agreed to what I suggested, which took a great weight from my mind.

That night I supped with the Governor in a great room, lined with rich tropical woods. The meal was excellent, and my host could not have been kinder in his manner. My thoughts, however, were not on the food, and I could not refrain from dancing a few steps in my excitement when at last I ascended the broad staircase to the sleeping chamber which had been prepared for me.

I waited as long as my patience would allow to give the other occupants of the house a chance to fall asleep. Then, with taper in hand, I stepped on to the balcony which ran the length of the house.

A low whistle from below, thrice repeated, told

me that Big Dixon was ready, as he had promised. Presently I heard a faint noise of something falling on my right, and I darted forward to find the end of a thin cord.

Cautiously I drew in the cord, hand over hand, and presently the end of a thick rope came into sight. This I fastened securely to one of the stanchions of the balustrade, then gave a whistle to signify that I was about to descend.

Big Dixon was below, ready to receive me.

"Well done, Dick," said I. "And now for our midnight visit to Morgan."

"I doubt if he'll be aboard his vessel," answered Dixon. "All the rum-shops are full of the buccaneers. I saw a man I thought was Morgan as I was on my way up, but there was no time for me to make certain."

"'Tis a pity, Dick, but we must chance it. Straight away for the quayside, and Morgan's vessel, is the word."

We kept to the side-streets as much as we could and in shadow. Every now and again we would stumble across some buccaneer, lying dead-drunk in the roadway, and once we found a hunched-up figure with a knife buried to the haft in his back. Port Royal was no place for saints in those days of Morgan and his buccaneers. Theft and murder were of daily occurrence.

We were about to emerge from a very narrow, very dark alley-way, when Big Dixon suddenly pressed me against the wall with a silent sweep of his great arm.

Hardly daring to breathe, I squeezed tightly against the wall, then, at a whispered command from Dixon, quietly moved back a dozen yards into the alley.

"Buccaneers coming," explained Dixon.

There were six in all, but instead of continuing along the broader road as we expected, they turned into the passage where we were concealed. However, they did not discover our presence, for they remained at the end of the lane. We caught the sound of subdued voices, and once the clash of steel. Evidently we had chanced upon a little gang with unpleasant work in hand.

Big Dixon nudged me, and I felt something hard pushed against my side. My trembling fingers closed round the butt of a pistol. This gave me confidence, and to be the more ready if fighting should occur, I drew out the knife I always carried in my belt.

The minutes dragged slowly past. Occasionally we heard mumbled voices from the ruffians, and found from their speech that they were Frenchmen. Although I could speak their language fluently, I could not hear much of what they said; but after a long silence I was suddenly thrilled by one of them crying, in a tense whisper, "He comes!"

We could see their dim forms arranging themselves ready to pounce out upon the unsuspecting man who was approaching. But to let murder or robbery be committed without lending a hand to prevent it was unthinkable. Therefore, just as we judged the proposed victim was some few yards from the entrance to the alley-way, Big Dixon let out a warning shout, to which I added my shrill treble.

It would have been wiser to have used our pistols right away, without stopping to ask questions, seeing that even if we reckoned the newcomer as a fighter on our side, we should still find ourselves sadly outnumbered. As it was, I thought at first that the surprised buccaneers were going to flee without seeing the numbers of those lurking in the shadows behind them. As the first few turned to run, one of them, apparently the ringleader, fired his pistol at random in our direction, then with a wild shout of "Let's kill Morgan first!" He leapt with naked blade, into the wider road.

His comrades turned at his cry, and rushed back to his aid. Shouts of rage and the clash of blades came to our ears.

"Come on, Dick!" I cried, though my big comrade, despite his wound, needed no prompting. He was out of the alley-way before me, his pistol cracked, and next moment one of the desperadoes was squirming on the ground.

I caught a quick glimpse of how affairs stood before joining the fray. Admiral Morgan, back to the wall, and a smile upon his broad face, was engaged in cutlass play with the five remaining buccaneers. But in spite of the long odds against him, he was very far from being content to defend himself. He slashed and cut as though thoroughly enjoying himself, while ever and anon he would make a swift thrust at one of his opponents, driving him backwards for a few yards then quickly leaping back again to his point of vantage.

Big Dixon, throwing down his empty pistol, grabbed one of the Frenchmen by the waist, meaning to toss him over his head. But Dixon's wound was not yet healed, and his strength failed him. The man he had gripped, dropping his cutlass, twisted himself round, and next moment he and Dixon had fallen to the ground, and were struggling savagely there.

Finding themselves attacked from the rear, the ringleader barked an order, at which one of his ruffians turned to confront me, leaving Morgan with three to fight. When my opponent realised he had a mere boy to contend with, a grin spread over his swarthy face, and he waved his cutlass playfully. Hurriedly I levelled my pistol at him, and fired, but my aim had been too hasty to be good, and the ball sped harmlessly by his ear. At this his grin grew broader, and he chuckled aloud when I flung the empty pistol at his head and again missed. I closed my eyes as I saw his cutlass swing upwards, but opened them again almost immediately, with the wild thought that I must do something to save my life, or who would there be to go in search of my father? For some reason or other I forgot the keen blade that I held in my left hand, and seeing nothing else for it, darted full at my opponent with lowered head.

It is a good job that my skull is an exceptionally thick one (my schoolmaster had told me this often enough in years gone by, little thinking how serviceable it was to prove in fighting, even if of little use in acquiring learning), for my head caught my antagonist such a shrewd blow in the stomach that he doubled up with the pain of it, and I myself tumbled backwards in a sitting position, blinking rapidly, and seeing more stars than those which lit up the sky.

My sudden onslaught, however, seemed likely to be of little service to me, for the French buccaneer, upon whose face an ugly scowl had appeared in place of the smile, turned to me with cutlass ready, eager to punish me for the blow I had dealt him. Before I could do anything to save myself, even had I possessed the power, Morgan came bursting through the men that beset him, and sent my assailant full length on the ground with a crisp blow of his fist upon the jaw. In a moment he had seized me by the neckerchief and swung me to my feet and against the wall. I found myself crouched down behind his back, whilst once again his blade clashed merrily with those that sought his life.

I suppose that if help had not arrived, the French buccaneers would have overcome Morgan, and killed us all, for Big Dixon still grappled with his opponent on the ground. Still, I am by no means sure. I never met the equal of Morgan as a fighter, and he might have won through despite odds against him. The matter was not put to the test. Before I had recovered my wits sufficiently to join once again in the fray, there came the clatter of running feet, and yells that told plainly enough of the approach of some of the English buccaneers. Our assailants, at least those able to depart, did not wait for our rescuers to arrive. They turned and fled like the wind; even the man wrestling with Big Dixon managed to wriggle free, and scamper off. There remained only the fellow that had been winged by Dixon's pistol-shot.

"Why, it's Admiral Morgan!" cried the big, black-bearded fellow that led the rescuing party. "We heard pistol-shots and thought there might be some fun."

"You came in good time, Black Jack," replied Morgan coolly. "If you take a dozen men with you quickly up the alley on your left, you may catch the rogues yet."

Black Jack waited for no more, but darted off in pursuit. Whereupon the Admiral turned to me, and began to thank me for my help. But the excitement, coupled with the blow on my head, had been too much for me. I tried to answer him but my tongue refused to work. A blackness fell before my eyes. I clutched for support, felt some clothes, lost them again, then, for a long while, I remembered no more.

CHAPTER IV

MY FLIGHT FROM JAMAICA

WHEN I came to, it was to find myself in a low room, dimly lit by a ship's lantern which hung from a hook in the centre. Big Dixon was bending over me, bathing my head with vinegar, while two or three other men, one of whom I recognised as the Admiral, were seated round a table, casting dice.

"Where am I?" I asked.

Hearing my voice, Morgan left the table and approached me.

"Well, my fighting bantam, feeling better?" he asked pleasantly.

"Yes, sir, thank you, though my head aches a little."

"Not half as much as the stomach of the Frenchie you butted," he responded with a great guffaw, and the others joined in his laughter in a way that showed me that my exploit had been told and enjoyed.

"'Twas the only thing to do, sir," I protested, blushing hotly. Doubtless seeing my embarrassment, Morgan hastened to ease the smart of the joke.

"Never fear, lad. All's fair in fighting, and but for your plucky rush, he'd have split you to the waist-band. And while I think of it, I must thank you and your big comrade for warning me of the Frenchies' ambuscade, and for your help in the fight."

"Nay, sir, 'twas nothing. And you certainly saved my life during the affair."

"I might not have been alive to save you, but for your warning, though I can assure you I'm pretty wary when I walk alone late at night. Well I know that many of the French buccaneers hate to think of me as their Admiral. Yet for the buccaneers to be strong enough to defy any great nation, they must combine, and whoever is chosen admiral must rule French and English alike. And, by Heaven, if the command is given me, as I think likely, I'll see that I am obeyed, or 'twill be the worse for the one who opposes me."

As he spoke he expanded his great chest, his voice swelled like the rolling of thunder, and his eyes grew terrible. I caught a glimpse in that moment of the dauntless spirit and fiery will that animated the man, and which was to enable him, in the years to come, to command effectively a force made up of as motley a crew of daring, treacherous, dare-devil ruffians as ever did great, seemingly impossible, feats of arms.

This fit soon passed, and he once again gave his thoughts to me.

"Aren't you the boy, Sir Hugh Ellis's son, who visited the Governor-General to-day?"

"Yes, sir. My father was taken prisoner, and——"

"I remember, lad. And there's something else I did not mention this morning. Your father and I were great friends in our younger days."

"Really, sir?" I asked. "But how——"

"Yes, my lad, I know what you were going to say. How comes it that your father, a trusted officer of the English Government, was once a friend of the notorious Harry Morgan, likely to be

Admiral of the Buccaneers? Ha, ha, ha! Never blush, lad, that I read your thoughts. Life plays strange tricks upon us. Once your father and I were officers together in the same regiment of horse in England. Now he is a knight, and but for his misfortune would be second-in-command upon this island. And what will be the fate of his once messmate, d'you think?"

I had not the slightest idea what to answer, but he evidently only asked the question for effect. With a merry twinkle of the eyes, and a thump upon the table that made the dice jump, he answered for himself.

"One of two things will happen to me, my lad. Either I'll be made a knight, like your father was, and I can tell ye that's a most unlikely possibility——"

He broke off to laugh heartily, and his comrades joined in uproariously at the thought of the English king knighting a buccaneer. When their laughter had somewhat abated, I managed to ask what was the other thing that might happen to him.

"My likely fate, lad, is to be strung up by the neck to my own yard-arm. At present, I know, the English authorities are friendly enough to the buccaneers. That's because we're useful to them in driving Spanish galleons from these seas. But wait until Spain and England are at peace again. Then it will be a case of combining forces to exterminate the buccaneers. However, we've our eyes open all right, and when that day comes, I, for one, shall have a store of treasure big enough to keep me in luxury for the rest of my days."

Feeling the time had come to fulfil the real business of my night's escapade, I made no attempt to answer Morgan's speech, which indeed was not addressed to me in particular, but was rather an utterance of his thoughts. After a little pause I asked him bluntly if I might join his ship's company.

His first impulse was to laugh, but at once he checked himself to ask me why.

"Because I believe my father's a prisoner, and I want to rescue him. The Governor-General wants to keep me tied to his apron-strings. I want to go where there's fighting with Spaniards, so that I may, perchance, learn news of my father's whereabouts."

"The lad's got spunk," said one of the men to Morgan.

"Ay," said another admiringly. "Let him have his way, Harry."

But Morgan looked very dubious. "I'd like to let you, boy, but is it wise? There's danger in plenty, be sure of that. And how can I take you away from the Governor?"

"As for danger, sir, as you knew my father well, you will expect his son to be prepared to run risks without flinching. And as for the Governor, let me know when you sail, and I'll guarantee to stow myself away on your ship, so that no blame can be given to you."

"You're the son of your father all right," agreed Morgan, with a chuckle, "but all the same——"

And so we argued for ten minutes, but all the time I felt that Morgan wanted me to join him though he pretended to oppose the project. In the end, at any rate, he let me have my will. He promised to take both Big Dixon and Fiddler Jim aboard his ship, and added that when he received orders to sail he would send one of my messmates, with instructions. Till that time I was to remain with the Governor-General, and if any news should come to hand concerning my father's fate, I was to send it along at once.

To say that I was elated is to use the mildest of language. I ran back home so fast that Big Dixon, who came to guard me, was taxed to the utmost to keep up with me. By the time we reached the Governor's house he was puffing and blowing like a grampus. I had to exert a tight control over myself or I should have sung aloud as I climbed back to my room. However, I managed to regain the balcony, fling down the rope to Big Dixon, and find my way to bed without any of the inhabitants of the house being the wiser.

Four days passed, and I began to wax impatient. I was athirst to be aboard with Morgan, sailing in search of my father. The thought that there might be vast difficulty in finding him did not occur to my boy's mind. It seemed quite a matter of course that we should attack and subdue some Spanish citadel, open the dungeons, and find there my father, hungry and weak, perhaps, but otherwise quite well. No wonder I chafed at the delay in carrying out this splendid dream.

During the period I was waiting for Morgan's message, I made shift to get what fun from life I could by playing tricks upon the tutor who had been engaged for me by the Governor. He was a tall, thin, earnest man, with rounded shoulders, and a head bent forward upon a long, thin neck. He had not the least idea how to keep a healthy youngster in order, and adopted a pleading attitude towards me which had not the slightest effect. In fact, it was so easy to play tricks upon him without the slightest chance of unpleasant consequences that the fun quickly palled, and I should have turned my attentions to other things had any presented themselves.

My tutor rejoiced in the name of Algernon Blackmore, and of course I called him "Algy," even to his face. Apple-pie beds, salt in his wine, stolen spectacles—he treated all these impish tricks in the same way, by addressing to me a few mild words of reproof which would not even have brought a blush to the cheek of a girl.

The evening that Morgan's message came, Algy had been very severe, for him. He had gone so far as to threaten to report me to the Governor on the following morning, a threat which worried me not a jot, for I knew he would never find the courage to put it into execution. When I bade him good-night before retiring to bed, I found him gazing at me with sad, forgiving eyes, and chuckled inwardly as I guessed his thoughts. Algy was convinced that I was thoroughly frightened, and was contemplating relieving my feelings by telling me he was going to forgive me.

"Are you really and truly sorry, Arthur?" he asked me gently

"Not a bit of it," I answered cheerfully. "Perhaps I shall be, of course, after I've had a thrashing from the Governor."

"If you say you're sorry, perhaps I'll——"

"I'm not sorry," I interrupted, for I had no wish to give him a loophole for abstaining from carrying out his threat; and with that I hastened off to bed.

I fell asleep almost at once. My dream of walking up and down the quarter-deck of a vessel of my own was suddenly interrupted by the shrill blast of a whistle from below. I was out of bed and had bundled on some clothes in record time. I could see down below the dim figure of a man.

"Is that you, Dick?" I whispered.

"Yes. We sail to-night. We've got to hurry to catch the tide."

"I'm ready, Dick. Heave up the rope."

In another minute I was hauling up the knotted rope by means of the cord Big Dixon had flung me. I had previously written a note to the Governor ready for when Morgan should send for me. In it I had stated my intention of running away to sea, whilst at the same time thanking him for his kindness to me. I did not say I was sailing in Morgan's ship lest he might have the power to call me back. This letter I hastily left on the pillow of my disordered bed, then, with one last look round, I climbed over the balcony rail, and slithered down the rope.

But instead of Big Dixon at the foot of it, I found a very excited, very nervous Algy.

"Oh, Arthur," he cried. "Fancy thinking I meant to report you. You poor child, to think of this."

"Why, sir, what—how—I mean to say——" I began, in my agitation.

"I know all about it, Arthur," said he, conjuring up a tender smile. "You knew I was going to report you, so you made up your mind to run away."

I was so flabbergasted by the poor fellow's foolish idea that words failed me.

"My poor boy," he went on, with that curious way he had of saying his words mincingly, as though they were coins that must be tested before delivery, lest some be under weight—"my poor boy, I did not mean to frighten you. I will forgive you everything."

Here was a quandary. How could I pretend to turn back, and make my real escape later, when Morgan's ships had to be away before turn of tide?"

"I'm not coming back," said I firmly. "I'm not running away because you threatened——"

But he cut me rudely short by flinging both his arms tightly round my neck. I cursed myself for my stupidity in not having dodged and run for it instead of attempting to argue. As it was, Algy had too good a hold upon me for there to be much chance of freeing myself. To make matters worse, he began to yell at the top of his shrill voice for aid.

I tried the manœuvre I had successfully played upon the French buccaneer. His grasp was too tight for me to succeed, and I only hurt my head against his chest. True there was a certain amount of satisfaction to come, for raising my head with a jerk, it struck him sharply on the chin, making him gasp painfully in the midst of one of his cries.

There was no time to waste. Already lights had appeared in the house. Very soon the doors would be opened, and soldiers or servants hastening to Algy's aid.

"Help, Dick, help!" I cried urgently.

Big Dixon, who had remained all this while under cover, uncertain how to act, did not fail me now. He loomed up out of the darkness, and Algy gave a little scream, like that of a frightened rabbit, as the sailor's great hands seized him round the waist, and swung him off his feet.

"What shall I do with the swab? Kill him?" demanded Big Dixon, while Algy squirmed miserably.

"Bring him with us. Then they'll not know what the alarm's for. As quick as you can for the shore!"

Swinging his frightened captive like a bag of oats across his broad shoulders, Big Dixon set off at a round pace, in spite of his burden, and I followed close in his wake. The streets were almost deserted, partly owing to the lateness of the hour, but chiefly because the bulk of the buccaneers were aboard their vessels, ready to sail with Morgan on his expedition. Of the few men we met, none attempted to bar our way, and we arrived at the quayside without any signs of the pursuit.

Big Dixon flung down his burden roughly in the bottom of the boat that was waiting for us. After lifting me in he gave the boat a tremendous heave which sent it yards from the shore, himself climbing in over the stern and calmly taking an oar.

The men aboard Morgan's ship were ready for us. Our boat was hauled aboard, and preparations made for an immediate departure. Big Dixon once more picked up my tutor, who lay as though unconscious, and bade me follow him to the Admiral's cabin.

On the way I caught sight of Fiddler Jim's grinning face. He touched his forelock in salutation, and lifted his violin meaningly. Soon after I heard strains of music swell into life, as he played a tune to which the men might work as they heaved away at the ropes. Rough voices sang the words, and the sound of tramping feet kept time to the merry tune.

Morgan bade us enter as soon as we knocked. He greeted me kindly, but looked rather surprised at Algy when Dixon flung him to the floor. I explained how it was that my tutor came to be aboard.

"Fling him overboard," ordered Morgan curtly. "We can't be worried by curs of his breed."

But I could not bear to think of the unlucky tutor being thus done to death, for I knew he was a poor swimmer. So I begged the Admiral to spare his life, which was contemptuously granted.

"But he's not to go snivelling about the ship," I was told. "Take him to the bos'n, Dixon, and tell him not to spare the rope's-end. Perhaps by the finish of our voyage we'll have knocked a little manhood into him."

Poor Algy was led off, looking woefully dejected, leaving me with Morgan.

"I've taken a fancy to you, my boy," said he, putting his hands on my shoulders, and staring into my eyes, "and I've made arrangements for you to keep near me. You'll sleep in a bunk I've had put up just outside my cabin, and it'll be your job to keep the cabin clean, and to fetch and carry for me. You'll not find me a hard master if you're spry and clean, but if you don't do your work well, you'll rue the consequences."

I was not displeased at the prospect, and promised to do my best. "You'll not forget my father, though, will you?" I asked. "My chief wish is to learn news of him."

"I'll not forget, lad. And now off to your bunk. You look tired, and you'll have plenty of work to do to-morrow."

But tired though I was, I could not fall asleep for many hours. The swing of the ship, the tramp and shouts of the men overhead, above all, the thought that we were adventure-bound, with a fair prospect of rescuing my father to boot, kept me awake for a long time. When sleep came at last, it was deep and dreamless.

Fiddler Jim woke me rudely the following day by hauling me out of my bunk.

"Is it cap'n you think you are?" he demanded. "The Admiral has been up these last two hours. He'll be down right away for breakfast, and you not ready to wait upon him."

Sleepily I thanked Fiddler for rousing me, and quickly ran on deck, there to dispel all remnants of slumber by dipping my head in a bucket of water pulled up from the sea. Hastily I dried myself, and ran below to tidy up the cabin before Morgan should appear. When he did arrive, some ten minutes later, he found everything ready for him, and myself prepared to wait at table.

Beyond a curt "Good morning," and an approving nod, he held no conversation with me until he had satisfied his appetite. That done, he bade me bring him his pipe and tobacco and settled down, with his feet propped up on the table-edge, for a quiet smoke.

I cleared away the remains of his breakfast, washed up the crockery, and put everything in its place. All the while Morgan watched me steadily, between gusts of tobacco smoke.

After being dismissed by the Admiral, I went on deck, anxious to examine the ship and to get to know some of the crew. Altogether there were nine vessels in the fleet destined to attack Porto Bello, and our own, as the Admiral's flagship (for Morgan had been definitely appointed in command of the fleet during the days I sojourned in the Governor's house), was in the van. It was a proud sight to see these noble vessels cutting their way through the gently heaving ocean before a breeze that filled the sails and carried us along at a fair speed. Yet it was a marvel that Morgan felt that the task of capturing Porto Bello was not impossible when he had so few vessels under his command, even though each was manned by fighters as fierce and desperate as the world had ever known.

As I gazed from the ship's side at her consorts, I heard a groan beside me, and turned to find my poor tutor lying on the deck. His face was the colour of foam, and there was ample evidence about him that the pitching and tossing of the ship had been overmuch for his stomach."

"Good morning, Mr. Algernon," said I cheekily, having, like most boys, but little sympathy for suffering.

Algy groaned.

"I wish I were dead!" he gasped, and in truth he looked as though he meant it.

"You wouldn't let me go, you know," said I, feeling sorry at last. "It was your own fault——"

"It was my duty to stop you. The Governor wanted—oh——"

He broke off suddenly, and held both his hands on his stomach in silent agony. It was funny enough, but I had now reached the stage of being very ashamed of myself for bringing Algy to sea. I watched him, not knowing how to comfort him, till he had somewhat recovered again.

"Can I do anything for you?" I asked. He replied by asking me a question in his turn. "Is there any way of getting back to dry land?" he inquired, in such a doleful voice that, despite my pity, I had to turn round to hide a laugh. Approaching us I saw Black Jack, the buccaneer I had met that evening Big Dixon and I had helped

Morgan against his French attackers. In his hand he held a knotted rope's-end, and a thrill of unpleasant anticipation ran through me, for this instrument usually meant pain for the ship's-boy. He greeted me with a friendly stare, however, and stood over Algy's prostrate body.

"What's the meaning of this, you swab?" he demanded fiercely, though there was more merriment than wrath in his eye.

"I'm sick—ill—dying!" complained Algy, and moaned.

"Well, you can't die here. Besides, you've made a mess on the deck, and that the Admiral can't abear. Best get a bucket of water and swab it away."

"But I tell you I'm dying——" began Algy. Whack! The rope's-end whistled through the air, and curled round the sick man's legs. Black Jack had not struck heavily, yet Algy gave a loud yell that brought a score of seamen to the scene.

"Now are you goin' to swab up that mess?"

Slowly Algy rolled on to all fours, but this laid him open to a more effective blow, which considerably hastened his movements. Finding the bos'n inexorable, Algy, with many groans, drew up a pail of water from the sea, and began to swab away the results of his own illness. The buccaneers around gave him all sorts of facetious advice, while Black Jack added an occasional touch with the rope's-end to keep him busy.

At last the deck was swabbed to the bos'n's satisfaction, but Algy was ordered to pull up yet another bucket of water. "What shall I do with this one?" he asked helplessly. "Put your head in it," was the brusque retort. Algy evidently thought this was not meant seriously, for he managed to conjure up a sickly smile, whereupon Black Jack, seizing him by the nape of the neck, forcibly ducked his head in the pail, and held it there for a good half-minute, while the hapless tutor's arms, legs, and body twisted in his frantic efforts to escape.

"Now get below, turn into your bunk, and don't let's have any more of this sea-sickness," grunted Black Jack. Spluttering and coughing, Algy made his way between the mocking buccaneers, being pushed from one to the other until I caught hold of him and led him below. At last I managed to get him in his bunk, where he lay, feebly moaning that he was dying.

But when four hours later he again appeared on deck, he tackled with gusto the smoke-dried meat and ship's biscuit the cook produced for him. And never again did he suffer from sea-sickness.

CHAPTER V

TROUBLE IN THE FLEET

A SPANISH galleon caught sight of us some twenty miles from Porto Bello. Round it turned, as though it had the devil behind it, and flew under full canvas to carry warning to the threatened port.

Morgan called a meeting of the skippers upon his flagship before Porto Bello came in sight. I was pleased to meet my old friend, Captain Gentle, whose ship, the *Hell-Fire*, was one of the fleet. A long conference took place in Morgan's cabin, and that night the Admiral told me the result of their deliberations.

"We all agree that we don't want to spend a long time bombarding Porto Bello. The longer we are, the more time they have to bring up reinforcements and sea galleons to cut off our retreat Pistol and cutlass shall take Porto Bello, not cannon-balls."

I asked him when he intended to launch his attack.

"To-morrow, at nightfall, my boy. Our boats will creep to the shore under cover of darkness, while our vessels fire a few broadsides as a blind. Every man that can be spared shall go in the boats. The Dons will never think of attempting to capture our ships, which need but a few men left to man them.

"And if our first assaults are unsuccessful, we have hopes that there is a traitor in Porto Bello who will help us take the place. He is an ex-priest, Knocker by name, who has long been in our pay. A cunning, treacherous fellow, and a bold one, to boot. Either he or one of his accomplices will be paying us a visit soon, possibly to-night. I want you to remain on deck, and if a rowing-boat approaches, hail it with the words 'Panama the goal!' The reply should be 'But Porto Bello first!' If the password is known, get the man aboard, and smuggle him down to me with as little fuss as possible."

Not till a full moon shone brightly in the sky did the object of my watch come into view. The ships had been hove-to, just out of sight of land, and lay like silver ghosts on the placid sea. The man who rowed the approaching boat was very slow and silent in his movements. He pulled close up to two of the other ships before he approached the flagship.

"Panama the goal!" I whispered cautiously, through cupped hands. For several seconds there was no reply, and I thought that either the rower had not heard me, or that he was not the man expected. Then came the answer, in a low, thick voice, "But Porto Bello first!"

With that the boat was rowed up under our stern and a thin rope was flung up to me, which I fastened to the rail. The mysterious visitor needed no help to ascend, climbing up the side like a wild cat.

He was the most unprepossessing fellow I had ever seen. Dark of skin, and powerfully built, there was a swagger and audacity in the way he bore himself which made me shiver. And his face was fiendish—no other word describes it. His eyes were bright and piercing, his chin resolute, and the leer that habitually played about his mouth was positively repulsive to see. But to mar whatever pretence he had to good looks, a white scar, relic of some cutlass fight, seared his face from nose to left ear. Yet with all his physical repulsiveness, on rare occasions when he wished to pose as an honest man, he could assume an air of benignity wondrous to behold.

"Well, boy, have you seen me well enough to know me again?" he asked in an ugly voice that well accorded with his unprepossessing appearance, at the same time gripping my shoulder so tightly that I almost screamed aloud.

"Yes, sir, I did not mean to stare," I managed to blurt out.

"But you did, eh?" And he gave me another twinge. "In future keep your eyes to yourself, or you may lose them. Who told you to challenge me?"

"Admiral Morgan, sir."

"Then lead me to him, and quickly."

Plucking a pistol from his belt, as thought to guard against possible treachery, he cocked it, then followed in my wake. Admiral Morgan bade me keep within call, and Knocker (as Morgan had greeted him) added that I was not to forget that keyholes weren't made to listen through. The two were closeted together for close on an hour, without interruption except upon one occasion when I was summoned to fetch wine and glasses. At the end of that time the Admiral and his visitor emerged from the cabin and went on deck, the former to set a fresh course for his fleet, the latter to drop down into his boat and pull away in the direction whence he had come.

"You're sailing away from Porto Bello, aren't

you?" I ventured to ask the Admiral when he returned to his cabin.

"Ay, boy, for so yon rascal advises. He is a cunning, nimble-witted rogue. He tells me that Porto Bello expects our attack, and that nothing but a surprise will take the outer fort. Therefore we are sailing to the westward, to hide ourselves in an anchorage I know of. Word will come to the Spanish Governor of Porto Bello that we have abandoned our project, a tale which will be readily believed, as the Dons think their port impregnable."

"Then how and when will you attack, sir?"

"In forty-eight hours' time. Knocker has had canoes hidden on the shore of our anchorage. We will man them and paddle along the coast, keeping close to land. The attack will commence early in the morning, and once we have taken the first and strongest fort, with certain suggestions from Knocker to help me I'll guarantee to take the other two, and sack the town."

Dawn found us in our new anchorage, and Morgan gave orders that most of the men might land for the day. I was one to take advantage of this command, and with Big Dixon and Fiddler Jim as bodyguard, and Algy in tow, lest he be tormented by the men if left on his own, I spent a happy couple of hours exploring the beach. Eventually the four of us settled down for a peaceful nap in a secluded cave we had stumbled against, Big Dixon, with a mighty effort, all but closing the entrance with a huge boulder to guard against disturbance.

High-pitched voices, in a strange tongue, dragged me loose from the bonds of sleep. It was some time before I could collect my wits sufficiently to realise that a number of men were talking excitedly just outside our cave. Then I caught Morgan's name, and a vile epithet, in French, attached to it. This finally banished all thoughts of sleep, and with noiseless step I made my way to the cave entrance, where I crouched behind the boulder which screened our hiding-place.

A meeting of the French buccaneers was in progress. Pierre the Red-headed, captain of one of the ships and a big man in the eyes of the French Brethren of the Coast, was addressing his fellow-countrymen with words of fire.

"Is there not wealth enough to be got from Spanish galleons?" he demanded. "What need have we to crack our heads against the walls of Porto Bello? We are not cowards, eh, but, mon Dieu, neither are we fools. Let us desert this English fool, this Morgan. If he wants to hang in chains, let him go to Porto Bello alone, he and his English pigs. For us the high seas and boardings—loot—life!"

His listeners applauded violently, and with excited gestures, as is the manner of Frenchmen. One, however, called out to know whether it was true that there was vast treasure at Porto Bello.

"True enough, mon ami, I expect. But what of that? Where is its final destination, I ask you? Why, Spain, of course. And how will it go to Spain? In galleons. And we shall take those galleons, is it not so, and the treasure is ours?"

"Why, then, does Morgan want to attack Porto Bello?"

"I will tell you, friend. There are two reasons. The Spaniards do not grant England's right to the possession of Jamaica, and plot to raise a force to retake it. This force is being built up at Porto

Bello. Therefore the Jamaican Governor, Monsieur Modyford, has commissioned Morgan to attack Porto Bello, and snuff out the Spanish plans—hey presto—like that!" And Pierre flicked together his thumb and middle finger.

"And the other reason, Pierre?" shouted one of the men.

"The other reason? Why, there are English prisoners in the dungeons of Porto Bello. One is an English nobleman of royal birth, I have heard it whispered. Therefore they must be rescued, eh? I ask you, my friends, would Morgan be so ready to lead the Brethren there if those prisoners were from our country, la belle France, eh?"

Roars of "No!" showed that he had his audience with him. Skilled leader of men that he was, Pierre knew when to change from words to action.

"Then let us show him that Frenchmen have wills of their own."

He strode dramatically away, and with cries of exultation his countrymen followed him. There was little time for me to think what to do. It would take Pierre and his party roughly a quarter of an hour to reach the shore of the anchorage opposite to which the ships were moored. If I could escape observation it might be possible to reach Morgan five minutes before them, and give him warning of the impending rebellion.

With a hurried kick at Algy to wake him from slumber, I set off at top speed, bearing to my left. This made the way longer, but for a considerable distance tall, dense bushes would separate me from Pierre and his men. Bruised and bleeding, panting for breath, I kept on my way as fast as weary legs would take me, and had the satisfaction of running up to where Morgan stood upon the beach before any of Pierre's party had arrived, and with sufficient breath left to blurt out what I had overheard.

Morgan's brow grew dark, and his lips drew together in a thin, straight line.

"The poltroons!" he exclaimed bitterly. "But I'm not surprised. Pierre is angry that he was not chosen Admiral of the Buccaneers. Jealousy, not cowardice, prevents him joining us in the attack on Porto Bello."

"What will you do?" I asked.

"Speak them fair. If they insist on deserting me, they must go, and take some of the ships with them. Whatever happens, I am determined to take Porto Bello!"

My admiration for Morgan grew tremendously in that moment. He had declared his intention of attacking Porto Bello. Had every man Jack of his fleet refused to follow him, I verily believe he would have gone on alone.

Before he could do more than call three or four of his most trusted captains to him, and charge them to prevent fighting between the rival parties of buccaneers, Pierre and his followers came into sight. They were excited and voluble, and as they approached, their ranks were swollen by others of their countrymen who had been absent when Pierre had made his speech. Nearer they drew, shouting to keep up their courage, some even waving naked cutlasses. And Morgan stood with arms folded on his great chest, and a sneer upon his handsome face.

Pierre halted some half-dozen yards in front of the Admiral, his hands resting nervously on the butts of his pistols. In spite of the knowledge that several hundred of his countrymen stood behind him, he was plainly ill at ease. As the rival leaders stood facing each other, a great hush fell upon the buccaneers, which neither of them was in a hurry to break.

I noticed that the English buccaneers, coolly and without haste, were forming up at a little distance behind their chief. Amongst them moved Captain Gentle, and other of the English skippers, urging upon the men not to commit any act of hostility.

"Well?" asked Morgan at length, and there was a wealth of scorn in his voice.

This single word was sufficient to unloose the flood of speech that Pierre had stored up. Volubly he repeated what I had heard him tell his French comrades. "We buccaneers are without country," concluded Pierre dramatically, "France, England, Holland—they are but names to us. Let our fighting be for our own good, to fill our pockets with pieces of eight. In the name of the Brethren of the Coast, Admiral Morgan, I call on you to abandon this mad scheme of attacking Porto Bello."

Loud yells of applause from the French buccaneers greeted the end of Pierre's speech. As for the Englishmen, they knew not quite what to think. Some of Pierre's arguments were plausible enough, and they had little loyalty for their native land. They kept silent, therefore, till Morgan should answer, and the Frenchmen also, anxious to know how he would reply, soon ceased their clamour.

"I could say a lot to you, Pierre, and those who think with you, but I'm not accustomed to argue. Nay, never dare to draw pistol on me, Pierre, or, by the sacred bards of Wales, I'll cut you in twain. Brethren of the Coast, are you, and fear to attack a place because there's a spice of danger? Clear off and be hanged to you! Quit buccaneering, and take to a monk's life—'twill suit you better, you——" and he finished with a string of oaths too horrible to repeat.

I myself shuddered at Morgan's fierce manner (for he was in a towering rage), though I was upon his side. Pierre turned his head this way and that, as though looking for some place where he might hide, and save himself from the Admiral's anger. You can imagine something of the awe which Morgan could instil into his followers when I say that not a single Frenchman aimed pistol to shoot him down, or waved cutlass in threatening fashion. As for the Englishmen, they cheered their leader to the echo, though he had advanced no arguments to counteract those offered by Pierre. His fiery words of scorn had done that which reasoned arguments might well have failed to do.

"Well, you scum, what are you waiting for?" roared Morgan. "Four ships I'll give you, not one more. You may take the——" and he reeled off the names of the four weakest vessels of his fleet. "Men on those ships who still intend following me, bring their belongings ashore. Those on other ships who wish to follow this sea-slug misnamed a buccaneer, take your gear aboard one of the vessels I've given him."

Pierre attempted to dispute Morgan's decision to allow him only four ships, but the Admiral turned on him like a mad bull. "You should go down on your knees and thank Heaven you escape with your life. You fool, d'you think I should let you go so easily if I didn't want to take Porto Bello more than anything else upon earth? Out of my sight, and if you're not out of the anchorage with your four ships by nightfall, not a single vessel shall you take away."

Pierre went, like a whipped schoolboy, and with him his men. From then, for two hours, there was a great going to and fro between vessels, for most of the Frenchmen elected to follow Pierre, and they had no wise to leave behind their belongings, which often included a secret bag of guineas. But the shuffling of men and kit was accomplished at last. An hour before sunset the four vessels weighed anchor, and slowly cleared the harbour, while Morgan's men lined the riggings of his ships to celebrate their departure with derisive cheers.

The following day Morgan ordered every man ashore, and told them his plans.

"True Brethren of the Coast," he began, "you know the task we have set ourselves. Yesterday you heard a craven say that it would pay us better to capture and loot Spanish galleons. How many Spanish galleons, think you, should we have to lay aboard before we collected such a store of wealth as shall be ours when we have captured Porto Bello? Fifty, say you? I tell you you could multiply that by fivescore, and still be wide of the mark.

"Brethren, with one day's fighting, I will make those that survive rich for life!

"But don't think it's going to be child's play. We've four hundred and fifty men left for the adventure. We must leave at least fifty to guard our ships; the rest will proceed in canoes. We'll paddle along the coast, and when we reach Porto Bello early to-morrow morning we'll find the Spaniards off their guard. They'll expect an attack in fighting-ships, if any attack at all. Once we're there it doesn't need me to tell you how to use cutlass and pistol."

It seemed a mad scheme to attack such a world-famed town as Porto Bello with scant four hundred men, after a long journey in frail canoes. But the men, who knew Morgan of old, cheered him to the echo, and none of them wanted to be assigned the post of guarding the ships. The worst fighters were selected for this job, amongst them Fiddler Jim, and of course Algy. I was the only one in the attacking party who was not a first-class fighting man, and that only by special permission of the Admiral, who knew how desperately anxious I was to glean news of my father. Big Dixon was given the task of looking after me during the fighting, and it was certainly pleasant to know that I should have this strong, brave Englishman at my side if danger threatened.

In all, twenty-four canoes set out upon the hazardous journey to Porto Bello. One was capsized within an hour of starting, and two of its crew drowned. This was a bad beginning, and augured ill for the success of our venture. Yet fortune was with us for the rest of the way in that, despite several patches of choppy sea, no other canoe was lost.

All through the afternoon the canoes were urged steadily along, hugging close against the shore. Once a Spanish galleon was sighted, far out to sea, but since our own craft lay so low in the water, we passed unobserved. The men relieved one another at the paddles every hour, and in spite of the slow rate at which we proceeded (for Morgan had no wish to arrive at Porto Bello with worn-out men), a few minutes' toil under the tropical sun made the men's backs glisten with sweat.

Darkness came, swift as ever, and the stars suddenly appeared in the sky. An evening breeze upblew that drove the heat away, and we made better progress. Hour after hour we paddled. My head drooped lower, and I slept.

Big Dixon woke me by gently shaking me. I found the canoes gathered together in a little group, and Morgan was giving last directions to his principal officers. Captain Gentle and a man called Scar-Face.

I looked towards the land, and saw white walls gleaming in the moonlight.

"Porto Bello," said Dixon, with a sweep of his great arm.

CHAPTER VI

NEWS OF MY FATHER

As Morgan had predicted, Porto Bello was unprepared for our attack.

Our fleet of canoes split up into three portions. That in the centre was under Morgan's own command. Captain Gentle, with seven canoes, was directed to attack on the right of the enemy's walls, Scar-Face on the left.

Cautiously we pulled for the shore. All was silent, so silent as to be almost ominous. The canoes were gently beached, and with all care the buccaneers disembarked, leaving one man in charge of each vessel. Light scaling ladders, made at the secret anchorage, and brought with us, were carried by the men to rear against the outer walls when the order came to scale them.

Morgan gave ample time for the other parties to gain their positions. While waiting to give the signal to attack, Morgan spread his men in dozens along the wall, a score of yards between each party. The signal was to have been a loud trumpet blast, but there came a crack of a musket from the left which showed us that some sentinel had kept good watch.

No need now for trumpet signal. With a wild yell that must have struck terror into the hearts of the half-awakened Dons, the ladders were propped against the walls, and up them swarmed the buccaneers. First of our party to reach the top was Morgan himself, bellowing a strange war-cry, and wielding cutlass like a light cane. After him went Big Dixon, then myself, and we found ourselves leaping down inside the defences to cross blades with bewildered Spaniards.

That first assault was easy work, and left the buccaneers jubilant, but anxious for more blood-letting. The surprise had been so complete that the Spaniards nowhere put up any defence worth talking about. Some turned to face us, and these were shot or cut down almost before they realised they were awake. Others, less bold or more far-seeing, immediately began to retreat to the second ring of the defences. Seeing this, Morgan followed hotly upon their heels, hoping to take the second fort before its defenders could properly organise themselves to beat us off. A few only of the buccaneers followed. The remainder were too intent on seeking plunder.

Morgan, with his dozen followers, pursued the retreating Spaniards so fiercely that he almost allowed himself to be taken. A Spanish grandee, probably the governor of the place, was organising the retreat with rare skill. Seeing Morgan and his buccaneers so close upon his heels, the Don gave a sudden order. Right about face swung his soldiers, their fire-arms were raised to their shoulders, and a scattered volley was fired at us.

"Down!" yelled Morgan, in a voice of thunder. Instinctively we flung ourselves to the ground, and the musket-balls whistled for the most part harmlessly in the air. The Spanish leader, unwilling that we should so easily escape, drew his rapier, and called upon his men to follow him. But Morgan was in his element when naked blades clashed in anger. Fiercely he met the Don's attack, his swiftly-moving cutlass proving effective guard against the foeman's point. And on Morgan's right hand stood Big Dixon, swinging a stout iron-bar as though he would never tire; while on the left Black Jack roared in his beard as he brought his foemen crashing down. The rest of Morgan's men also fought valiantly, so that the Don thought he had more to lose than gain by continuing. So he gave a swift command, and away he and his men doubled to rejoin their main party, which had continued to retreat. Finding himself with so few supporters, Morgan gave up the chase, and returned to the outer wall to form up his men, and reckon up his casualties.

These latter were remarkably few. Two men killed, and a number of minor wounds, made up the sum of our losses.

Quickly Morgan gave his orders, and put into operation the fiendish plan that later I found had been suggested to him by the inhuman Knocker. While three hundred of the buccaneers were kept under arms ready to meet any sortie by the Spaniards, the remainder were split up into two parties. One of these was given the task of fashioning broad ladders, up which four or five men could climb abreast. The other party was ordered to round up the nuns and monks who had fallen into our hands, for as Morgan said, grimly humorous, "It is the duty of religious folk to lead the way for infidels."

I guessed his cruel purpose. Big Dixon confirmed my fears. "He's going to march yon poor folk in front of his buccaneers," he said. "If the Spaniards fire, they'll be shooting down their own women and priests."

How I hate to remember the ghastly business that followed! The priests and nuns were formed up in front of the buccaneers, and at pistol-point driven towards the walls of the second fort. Behind them were carried the wide ladders, and by using the religious folk as a shield, the buccaneers contrived to rear their ladders against the walls without loss.

The Spanish soldiers had not fired upon their country-folk, and now their Governor appeared upon the wall, under cover of a flag of truce.

"Well?" demanded Morgan, boldly stepping forth. "Do you wish to surrender."

"Never!" replied the Don resolutely. "Am I speaking to the commander of your forces?"

"You are."

"May I ask what these priests and nuns are doing here? May I request you to send them back to safety, so that we may fight it out between ourselves?"

"You may ask, Señor, but I am afraid we cannot agree unless you have good reasons for what you require."

"Reason enough, Señor Buccaneer. We do not war on women."

"Indeed," replied Morgan, his eyes flashing. "Yet I had a sister who fell into the hands of your Holy Inquisition. They tortured her, poor girl, and in the end burned her at the stake. Was not that warring on women?"

For a moment the Governor made no reply, but at length he said, "What the Holy Inquisition does, it does with a reason. Its object is to save souls, even though it must kill bodies to do so. You have no such reason. I appeal to you to send back those priests and nuns to safety."

Morgan flung back his head and laughed long and bitterly.

"I've reasons for what I do, I assure you, Señor Governor. To save the lives of my buccaneers I'm willing to sacrifice the bodies of these nuns and priests. So under cover, and quickly, for we are about to fire."

"The sin be on your head, then," replied the Spaniard, and disappeared from view.

And now there broke forth a fierce fire from the defenders, and many of the hapless priests and nuns fell moaning to earth. But there were many more to take their places, and these were pushed forward, and forced to climb the broad ladders, five abreast, in face of their countrymen's fire. Dozens of them fell, but still no pity was shown by the buccaneers, who eventually gained a footing upon the walls, having suffered but few losses, thanks to their living shelter.

A footing once accomplished, the rest of the buccaneers swarmed up the ladders to their comrades' support. Howling like wolves, they flung themselves at the defenders, though these far exceeded them in numbers. Foremost of all went Morgan, yelling encouragement to his men, and setting them an example of reckless courage by his own deeds. The huge bulk of Captain Gentle could be seen hacking its way amongst the foe. Scar-Face, small but reckless, sprang hither and thither like a wild cat. Black Jack fought without fury, but in grim earnest, and few cared to meet him face to face. None of the buccaneers, indeed, but fought as though he enjoyed it, and as though the possibility of defeat was unthinkable.

For their part the Spaniards, led by their gallant Governor, put up a splendid resistance. Well they knew what mercy they might expect if they surrendered. They had seen pale-faced nuns and heroic priests fall before their own fire, and the sight had infuriated them. Also they knew their numbers to exceed those of the assailants, though probably they little guessed that Porto Bello was being taken by a mere four hundred men.

The fighting, then, was for a long time desperate and evenly-balanced, and each of our party was called upon to bear himself manfully. Boy though I was, I kept in the forefront of the buccaneers, eager to attack the Spaniards. My first opponent was armed with a long pike, which he thrust fiercely at my chest. My nimbleness stood me in good stead, for I ducked quickly. The very fierceness of the blow brought about the Dons' ruin, for he could not keep his balance, and as he pitched forward, I struck with all my strength at the nape of his neck.

"Well done, Arthur!" came Big Dixon's hearty voice, as he took upon his cutlass a blow aimed at me, and cut down the wielder with a swift return. "If you're hard-pressed, don't forget your pistols."

The advice was to prove useful. So far as he could, Big Dixon kept close beside me, fighting my antagonists as well as his own. But in the press and flurry of the conflict, we were separated, and I found myself beset by two Spaniards, one a huge fellow, who looked almost as strong as Big Dixon himself. This giant aimed a downward blow at me that I only just avoided by a swift, backward leap. Again he struck, and there was no time to dodge. I was saved, by a strange freak of fate, by my other opponent, who chose that moment to run at me with dagger drawn. The blow meant for me fell upon his steel helmet, and down he fell. Before my huge opponent could recover his weapon, which had been torn from his grasp by the force of the blow, I had plucked a pistol from my belt, and fired at point-blank range.

Excited at my success, I ran towards the spot where the fighting raged fiercest, but before I reached it I slipped upon a patch of blood, and fell headlong. There came an excruciating pain in my left ankle, and when I tried to rise to my feet, I found myself scarcely able to stand.

Fortunately for me the fighting had moved from my vicinity. At first I lay, faint from the pain of my hurt ankle. When I felt somewhat better, I decided to crawl to some less exposed spot, from which I could watch the progress of the conflict.

I pulled the second pistol from my belt, and saw that it was primed and cocked. With this in my right hand, I started my painful journey towards the remains of a high wall some twenty yards to my left.

Many dead bodies lay in my path, mostly Spanish, with here and there a buccaneer. One of the Spanish bodies I touched turned round, and seeing my dress, the man, though wounded to death, clutched me by the throat so suddenly that I dropped my pistol, unexploded. But the effort had been too much for the Don. His fingers relaxed, and his body sank back. One last look of hatred, and his eyes glazed with death.

I reached the wall at last, but while I was attempting to climb atop of it, Big Dixon came running up to me, his honest face looking frightfully woebegone in his fear that I had been wounded. He gathered half a dozen of undischarged pistols from the dead men around, so that I should be able to defend myself if attacked, and promised to keep an eye upon my hiding-place and bring help if I signalled.

From my point of vantage I was able to see most of the fighting still in progress. The buccaneers continued to press savagely, while much of the fire had gone out of the Spanish resistance. Had it not been for the desperate example of the Spanish Governor I am certain there would have been a hurried withdrawal to the third fort.

Admiral Morgan realised that the Spanish resistance would collapse once the Governor was slain, and set out to meet him face to face. As though by mutual consent, Dons and buccaneers drew back from their respective leaders, leaving the twain to meet each other on open ground.

The Don was a man of medium size, clad in corselet and helmet of steel, and armed with a long sword which had more than once pierced deeply into enemy flesh. Morgan, large but active, wore no armour, and fought chiefly with cutlass, though he carried a sharp dagger in his left hand for close fighting. For a moment or two the rival leaders gazed at each other, as though measuring the skill of his opponent, then the Spaniard threw himself on guard, and Morgan upswung his heavy weapon.

The Admiral nearly lost his life in the first few passes. Leaping sideways to avoid a lightning thrust, he missed his footing, and fell to the ground. Like a flash the Spaniard rushed in, and thrust fiercely. Somehow Morgan managed to ward off the blow with his dagger, and, with an agility marvellous in so heavy a man, he leaped to his feet, cutlass ready.

The Spanish Governor was a wonderful swordsman, and had he been opposed by a similar weapon no doubt victory would have been his. But the coarser methods of cutlass fighting put him at a disadvantage, for Morgan was so active that it was difficult to reach him, and his blade swung to and fro so swiftly as to make his defence almost impregnable.

Once Morgan dropped to one knee, and, with a shout of triumph, the Spaniard drew back his sword arm to make the fatal thrust. As his weapon flashed forward, up swung Morgan's cutlass blade, catching the Governor's wrist from beneath, severing hand from body.

Courageous to the end, the Spaniard picked up his sword in his left hand and sprang at Morgan's throat. It was a desperate effort, and failed. The buccaneer did not attempt to avoid the rush. Standing sturdily, with feet apart, he swung his cutlass in the air, holding it with both hands to give the more strength to his blow. I closed my eyes in time to avoid seeing the heroic Governor cut down.

With the loss of their leader, the Spanish resistance gave way. Back streamed the survivors, eager to take shelter in the third fort. After them rushed the buccaneers, hacking and hewing savagely, until Morgan's stentorian voice bade them desist.

"Time enough for capturing the third fort to-night," said he. "There won't be any difficulty in taking that. For a few hours there's looting to be done. Search the houses, and bring the treasure you find to the market square. No man is to steal for himself, mind. All the plunder will be divided according to rank when the fighting is over. Our comrades guarding the ship are to have equal shares with the rest!"

"What about the townsfolk, Admiral?" roared

one of the men. "We can do as we please with them, eh?"

"So long as you use your wits about it. Many a fat citizen will have buried his little hoard in some secret place. No use in killing such a one till he has given up his secret. A little torture, skilfully applied, will often open unwilling lips. And no drunkenness till the place is ours. Any man unfit to attack the third fort to-night on account of liquor shall swing for it. You know me for a man of my word."

"Ay, ay, Admiral!" With that the rogues departed, and with their leaders to direct them, began a systematic looting of the town. Many sights I saw that day that filled me with loathing for the cruelty of these buccaneers. Yet it is only fair to remember that they were but returning to the Spaniards the same sort of treatment they had previously had to endure at the Dons' hands.

Big Dixon left the looting and the torturing to the other buccaneers and devoted himself to my business. His first task was to bandage my sprained ankle, and soak it with cold water, and let me say at once that though I suffered considerable pain, and was for several hours unable to put foot to earth, before three days had passed the ankle was quite recovered.

Never once during the attack on Porto Bello had I forgotten my object in joining the ranks of the buccaneers. With Big Dixon to help me, we began our search for wounded Spanish soldiers who might have some knowledge of English prisoners in the forts.

There were few enough wounded, for the buccaneers slew any Spanish soldiers they found, well knowing that these would have no concealed treasure. Diligent search found us a few, but at first we could learn no news of any use to us. But presently we found a young Spaniard, unwounded but scared to death, who had taken refuge in a disused well.

At our appearance he fell to babbling for mercy, although we made no effort to hurt him. In spite of our assurance that we intended him no harm, he still made so much uproar that I feared he would attract the attention of some of the other buccaneers, who would likely seize him to serve them for sport. When at length we dragged him from the well, he fell to his knees, and flung his arms imploringly round Dixon's legs.

"Why, 'tis a mermaid we've laid hold of by the way its arms are ready to embrace an honest seaman," cried Dick, dealing the poltroon a smart blow upon the head.

"Shoot the fool if he can't keep quiet," said I, imitating Morgan's manner, but belying my words with a significant wink.

Big Dixon clapped a pistol to the man's head, whereupon he relaxed his hold, and instead fell a-blubbering.

"Silence, man," said I, speaking as before, in Spanish. "You've only to answer a few questions truthfully to escape all hurt."

With that he ceased his blubbering, and excitedly offered to answer any questions we liked, if only we spared his life. Finding him so ready, I asked him if he knew of any captured English ship entering Porto Bello during the last fortnight.

"But yes, Señor. A very battered, battle-worn schooner came limping into port just about a week ago."

"What was her name?" I asked excitedly, feeling I was on the right track at last.

"Alas, Señor, that I cannot say, though I heard it at the time. But I can describe her figure-head. A woman, with long, fair hair, playing a harp and——"

"'Tis she! The *Rover!*" I exclaimed. "Tell me more. Were there any prisoners aboard her?"

"*Rover?* Yes, that is the name, I think. And prisoners, Señor? Yes, close on a score. One, they say, was an English knight, taken on his way to Jamaica, to be governor there."

"Was he a tall man, slightly lame of his right leg? Square shoulders? Grey hair? Light blue eyes?"

"The very same, Señor. I saw him several times, for my father was gaoler of the dungeons, and often bade me take meals to the prisoners."

"Where is he, then? Quick, tell me. Is he in the third fort?"

"Alas, Señor, the knight and his comrades are no longer in Porto Bello. They left three days ago."

"Where have they gone? Quick, man, tell me all you know."

With that he explained that on the approach of the buccaneer fleet, the Governor had ordered all prisoners to be sent away. Some had been sent to Maracaybo, and others across the isthmus to Panama. But in which party my father had been sent he could not tell, as the prisoners were making the first stage of the journey in one body.

Disappointed though I was, I rejoiced exceedingly to learn that my father had survived the boarding of the *Rover*. That he was a prisoner in Spanish hands was sad news enough, but I swore again to myself that I would do all in my power to free him.

We let our prisoner free by escorting him through the town to the outskirts, and there letting him loose. The youth thanked us heartily for his deliverance, and promised, with tears in his eyes, that he would repay our kindness if ever the opportunity occurred.

Just before he left us it struck me that he might be able to bear a message to my father, and he willingly promised to do his best. I had paper with me, but no ink for writing, so I burnt a piece of wood until it had changed to charcoal, and with that scrawled a few words to say that I was well, and would seek him out. In addition to this written message I bade the Spaniard add by word of mouth that I was in the best of health, and hoped to meet my father again soon. Then giving the youth one of my pistols for his protection I watched him disappear amongst the trees of the forest that bordered that side of the town, my eyes full of tears.

"Cheer up, comrade," quoth Big Dixon, willing to hearten me.

"Alas, Dick, I would I were that messenger, that I might see my father's dear face again. How many months, years maybe, will it take me to seek him out and rescue him?"

CHAPTER VII

THE SACK OF PORTO BELLO

It was midnight before Morgan marshalled his men for the final onslaught to make Porto Bello completely ours.

The moon, which was full, ever and again was hidden by thick banks of cloud. But when it did shine forth unobscured, all was as bright as day.

Despite the freedom given to the men, none was the worse for liquor, which told me much of the power Morgan wielded over the buccaneers. All were eager for the attack on the third fort, and each boasted how many Dons he would slay.

"Stubborn lot of fellows, these citizens," quoth one, as he and his comrades waited for the order to attack. "I wanted one of them, a shopkeeper, to show me where he had hidden his wealth. Swore he had none, the rogue, so I chopped his fingers off, one by one, till he told me. Not till I'd cut off three did he squeal what I wanted."

"And what then, Jem?"

"I made him dig up what he'd hidden, then shot him and buried him in the same hole," answered Jem, amid the rough laughter of his fellows.

"That reminds me," chimed in another. "A fat, greasy little fellow swore that he was a pauper, and had no hoard stored snugly away. So I tied him up by his waistbelt to the bough of a tree, and lit a slow fire under him to help warm up his memory. And, split my sides, comrades, if I didn't forget all about him. He'll be swinging there still, like an overdone fowl."

Disgusted at their devilry, I limped away, Big Dixon following me, out of earshot of the scoundrels. We sat ourselves down upon a stone wall, feeling sick at heart that fate had made it necessary for us to fight side by side with the Brethren of the Coast.

As we sat awaiting the signal for the assault, of a sudden Big Dixon laid his great hand warningly upon my knee, pointing with his forefinger down the narrow road in which we sat.

At first I saw nothing untoward, for the moon was in hiding. Presently, as my eyes searched the shadows, I saw what Dixon's sharper eyes had previously detected, a misty figure coming towards us.

A clutch at my shirt-sleeve warned me to get under cover. Big Dixon motioned me to shelter behind his broad back, and thus we both crouched, waiting for the newcomer, who crept along cautiously.

Big Dixon drew a pistol from his belt, an example I quickly followed.

The intruder had passed our hiding-place before Big Dixon stepped forward and challenged him. "I've got you covered. Put up your hands or I fire!" warned Dick.

The unknown, who was enveloped in a long cloak slowly did as he was told, but remained with his back towards us. Dixon strode forward and swung the man round to see who he was.

It was a foolish move. The stranger's uplifted hands closed like a vice about my comrade's pistol hand. Next moment the two of them were on the ground, snarling like fighting wolves, and rolling one over the other with astonishing rapidity.

I had seen Big Dixon fight on several occasions previously, and never before had his strength been seriously challenged. Yet here he appeared to have met his match. The stranger was indescribably swift in his movements, and tremendously powerful in spite of his inferior size. Eventually he managed to hold Big Dixon, back downwards, on the ground, with a curious hold that needed but one arm to secure the giant, his own body lying at right-angles to Dixon's.

During the fight, while the two combatants had been too busy to realise my presence, I had picked up my comrade's fallen pistol and had tried in vain to put myself in a position where I could cover the stranger without fear of hurting Dixon. I felt that now my chance had come, and was spurred to act the faster by the unknown snatching a knife from his belt and raising it aloft to strike. While the blade still flashed in the moonlight (the moon having climbed from behind the clouds) I stepped briskly forward and clapped the pistol behind the stranger's ear.

"Strike, and I fire!" cried I.

At that he turned his face towards me, and I beheld with fear and loathing the same evil, scar-crossed face I had seen aboard Morgan's ship. It was the spy, Knocker.

He scowled fiercely as he saw me, nearly making me drop my pistol in fright. With an effort I kept calm, for I knew not what his motives were in thus creeping along the streets, and judged it better to keep him covered until we knew whether he meant harm to us.

"Put that pistol down, fool!" he snarled, with a curse.

I thought it better to speak him fair, but all the same I did not obey his command. Instead, I asked him civilly enough what he wanted, at the same time requesting him to let my comrade rise. This he did, very ungraciously, and pushed his knife back into his belt.

"'Tis Morgan I'm after," he growled, still scowling evilly. "What d'you mean by setting on me in this fashion, you great bullock, you?"

"Why, friend," replied Big Dixon amiably, "I wanted to see who you were and whether you bore an honest face. However, since my young friend here knows you, we'll take you to Morgan in spite of it."

"In spite of what, oaf?"

"Your honest face, comrade," and Big Dixon shook with laughter at his own joke. As for Knocker, I thought he meant knifing Dixon, and grasped my pistol the firmer in readiness to help. He apparently thought better of it, and curtly bade me to lead him to Morgan, adding that he did not want to be seen by the other buccaneers.

Morgan was delighted to see his visitor, whom I introduced into the room he had chosen as his headquarters.

"Welcome," said he. "In half an hour from now I should have started the attack. What makes you late?"

"It was risky work leaving the fort for one thing. For another, these two fools have delayed me for a quarter-hour. Perhaps you'll see they're punished."

I began to protest at this, but Morgan stayed me with a gesture. "I'll hear what you have to say in the morning. For the present, Dixon, you may go. Arthur, bring us wine and clean glasses."

"Well?" asked Knocker, as he drank. "Have I served you well, as yet?"

"Your information was quite correct, and your suggestion for capturing the second fort admirably successful. If only your promise to help us take the third and strongest fort is carried out, to-morrow will see our red cross flying in place of the Spanish flag."

"And the price? You remember our bargain?"

"Ten thousand pieces of eight! You shall have them, never fear. I'll squeeze treble that sum from the Spaniards to make us evacuate the town."

"And command of a vessel in your fleet. That was part of the bargain. I'm tired of masquerading as a priest ashore here. You'll find me a useful captain."

"And a dangerous," thought I to myself, watching his crafty eyes. But Morgan seemed not to sense his villainy.

"Captain you shall be, Knocker, and long may we both live to fight against the Dons. And now, what about your promise? Can you blow up the powder magazine as arranged?"

"It shall be done. Lead on your men at dawn. In the bustle and confusion of the defence I shall easily set fire to the trail already laid in the magazine. But see that none of your rogues fall upon me when the place is in your hands."

"Never fear, Knocker. Wear your priest's rig, and remember the watchword 'Mansvelt.' That will save you should any of my buccaneers feel inclined to knife a Spanish priest."

They talked for another ten minutes, perfecting their arrangements, then Big Dixon and I were given the task of guiding Knocker in safety through the streets leading upward to the third fort, since there might be danger from buccaneers, or from any of the townsfolk who had survived the day's massacre. He did not condescend to talk to us on the way, and we were both very pleased to see the back of him.

Dawn came, quick and beautiful, and so the buccaneers, bearing their scaling-ladders, pushed forward to the attack. The Spaniards in the fort were on the look-out, and immediately the clang of beaten metal sounded the alarm along the walls, and the roll of drums called the soldiers to arms. Concentrated and effective musket-fire greeted our appearance in the open space leading to the walls, and many of the assailants dropped in their tracks.

Undaunted, the buccaneers pushed on at a brisk double, as though heedless of the galling fire. When one of the men was shot down, another took his place without fuss. Those who bore no burdens dropped occasionally to their knees, and directed an accurate fire against any Spaniard who ventured to show his head above the walls.

No sooner were the walls reached than the ladders were tilted against them, and dauntlessly the buccaneers began to climb to the assault, as though revelling in danger. The effort of the defenders became more desperate than ever. Huge boulders, molten lead, and lumps of metal were cast down upon us, in addition to the musket-fire and a rain of arrows. But so accurate was the marksmanship of the buccaneers covering with their fire those scaling the ladders, that severa shot Spaniards fell amongst the other missiles upon the heads of the attackers below.

It is difficult to predict how the fight would have ended, had it not been for Knocker's treachery. Desperately and fearlessly though the buccaneers advanced to the assault, their numbers were vastly inferior to those of the defenders.

As it was, the buccaneers had a powerful ally within the walls of the fort. While the fighting was at its height, there came a sudden blinding flash which for a minute dazed every eye, followed by a great explosion that shook the fort and the very ground under our feet. Even I, who expected such an event, was stunned by the terrific nature of the explosion. How much more, then, must it have daunted the Spanish defenders, as they gazed fearfully behind them to behold a cascade of falling stones?

Morgan was quick to take advantage of this surprise.

"Forward!" he cried, and "Forward!" echoed Captain Gentle, Scar-Face, and others of the captains. They themselves set a splendid example by dashing up scaling ladders and reaching the battlements whilst the Dons were still stunned by the unexpected disaster.

With loud huzzas the buccaneers followed. Too late the Spaniards turned once again to the fight. We were upon them, our pistols cracking at point-blank range, our cutlasses swinging merrily. The heart had gone out of our foes. The sight of Captain Gentle hewing his way through their ranks, of Scar-Face yelling oaths each time he cut down an opponent, of Big Dixon towering above their heads and laying about him with a stout iron bar, and, above all, of Morgan, with fierce eyes, setting a wonderful example to his men, was too much for them. Some began to run wildly, hither and thither, vainly seeking safety. Others fell upon their knees, yelling wildly for mercy from men who granted none. A few still fought on, doggedly but without hope, until they were pistolled or cut down. Of all those remaining upon the wall, not one was knowingly spared.

Resistance over, the buccaneers scattered, happy as schoolboys enjoying a game, in search of Spaniards in hiding. All who were found were dragged out and either immediately slain or tortured to satisfy the cruel lusts of their victors.

I tried to find Morgan, to persuade him to spare as many of the Dons as he could, partly because I wished to learn more news of my father and the other survivors of the *Rover's* crew, but chiefly because I was sick to death of seeing the ruthless treatment meted out to the unfortunate Spaniards. Morgan was not to be found, however, having taken a picked body of his men in search of the treasure-house. Therefore I called upon Big Dixon to aid me, and set out to obtain what information I could from any of the Spaniards who still survived.

Our path led us towards the spot where the explosion had occurred. Here there was now a large crater, with blackened sides, while broken-down walls and still-smouldering rafters marked where the exploded powder had been stored.

Leaning against a pile of débris on the farther side of the crater was a man, clad in the garments of a Spanish priest, calmly smoking. "Knocker!" I whispered to my comrade, and we crouched down behind the ruins of a wall, having no wish for further dealings with the traitor.

As we watched, two of the buccaneers, carrying naked blades dyed with blood, came swaggering along, still enjoying their hunt for other Spaniards to kill. Catching sight of the supposed priest, they uttered a yell of exultation, and hastened along. Perhaps they had forgotten Morgan's explicit instructions that no priest should be injured, until he had been given the challenge word, "Death to Spaniards!" to which the reply should be, as Knocker had been told, "Mansvelt!" At any rate, they gave no challenge, but one of them prodded him with the point of his cutlass, while the other looked as though he intended cutting him in twain.

Knocker made no attempt at explanation. Out came his hand, which had been hidden against his breast, and in it was a pistol. This he pointed full at the fellow whose blade had touched him, and pressed the trigger. For a moment I thought the bullet had missed, for the man remained standing; but presently he clasped both hands upon his chest, swayed to and fro like a man in a trance, then fell heavily, face downward.

His comrade, with a snarl, dashed forward to avenge his death. Upwards swung his blade. It had begun its downward sweep, and still the pretended priest had not moved. At the last moment Knocker sprang in under the other's arm, so that the twain stood breast to breast. A knife blade flashed in the sunlight. Without a cry the second buccaneer fell.

"Come away!" whispered Big Dixon huskily. "Yonder is no man, but a fiend. Let us hope he never serves alongside Morgan. Heaven knows what cruelties he will inspire." So we crept silently away.

And now there followed at Porto Bello several days of such wild debauchery as disgusts me to remember. Once the buccaneers had collected together, and stored upon their ships (which had been brought to Porto Bello) all the treasure they could find, they gave themselves up to feasting and drinking on such an outrageous scale that it was no uncommon thing, night or day, to find scores of the buccaneers lying too drunk to be aroused, sometimes in the very puddles of the street.

Why did Morgan not keep his men under better control? That he could enforce discipline no one could deny. I think that it suited his purpose after such severe fighting to allow his men a period of wild pleasure. They would fight all the fiercer on a subsequent occasion, in the expectation of a like reward.

But the Admiral was too experienced a commander to run the risk of a surprise attack. All the time he occupied Porto Bello he kept a large number of men sober, and under arms. Two galleons, day and night, scoured the ocean, beyond the sky-line, on the look out for enemy ships. Picked bands of men kept watch in outposts, a day's journey from the town, to bear word should any enemy force approach by land. Morgan had no intention of being caught napping, as the Spaniards had been.

I still carried on my duties of cabin-boy, and as often as not had to wait upon Knocker as well, who was in high favour with the Admiral. This traitor had conceived a violent dislike to me, which was as violently reciprocated. Almost directly he had joined us as a Captain of Buccaneers he picked upon some fancied carelessness of mine as an excuse to thrash me with a rope's-end. He had given me one stinging blow across the shoulders when Morgan appeared, and angrily bade him desist. After that he made no more attempts to hurt me physically, but did so in a dozen other ways by his sneers. What hurt me most of all was the idea that he was setting Morgan against me, for I had great faith that through the admiral I should be able to rescue my father.

One evening, as Fiddler Jim sat upon an upturned keg, playing sea shanties to such of the buccaneers as were sober enough to listen to him, there came a man running at a jog-trot (though near to dropping from very weariness), who fell as he reached the circle of men that ringed the fiddler round. Rough hands ministered to the worn-out runner. A pannikin of rum was put against his lips. Algy, who had already lost much of his effeminacy, dipped cloth in water and wiped the sweat and grime from the runner's face. Revived by these attentions, he staggered to his feet, and asked for Morgan.

"Quickly! quickly!" he urged. "A Spanish force is on its way hither from Panama!"

The Admiral came hastening forth at this news. There was an immediate call for his officers. All men who were sober were marshalled together at once, and given the task of seeing that no more liquor was supplied to their drunken comrades. The messenger stated that the Spanish force consisted of between two and three thousand men, well armed. They were travelling at a fairly slow rate, owing to the difficulty of transport. His companions at the outpost which had seen the approach of the avenging force would retreat slowly before it, keeping it under constant observation. Men had already been sent to tell the other outposts to fall back upon Porto Bello.

"Two or three thousand, eh?" said Morgan, "and we've over three hundred fighting men. There's no need to worry about retreat."

Nor did he. When, two days later, the Spanish force appeared in front of Porto Bello, every buccaneer had recovered from his debauch and was in fighting trim, ready to die in the defence of the town which had been so daringly captured.

But there was no fighting, after all. The Spaniards sent forward an envoy, under a flag of truce, who was admitted to Morgan's presence. I was bidden to bring wine, and I took the opportunity of remaining (under the pretence of ministering to their wants), and thus I heard nearly all that was said.

At first the Spanish officer tried to carry off matters with a high hand, demanding the submission of the whole buccaneer force. Morgan laughed at him and asked him whether he thought that the buccaneers who had been bold enough to capture Porto Bello would not be able to defend it. There followed further discussion, and presently the Spaniard offered, as though granting a favour, to allow the buccaneers to withdraw to their ships unmolested. Again Morgan laughed.

"Why talk like a child, Señor? We have all the treasure we can find in Porto Bello safely aboard our ships. We could have sailed away days before your troops came in sight. Do you think I stopped just for the pleasure of drinking wine with you? No, Señor, though"—and here he bowed—"it is certainly an honour. We are stopping in Porto Bello until we are pushed out, which you will find no easy task, or until we are paid, and paid handsomely, to evacuate."

In the end Morgan gained his way. No less than one hundred thousand pieces of eight were handed over to the buccaneers for quitting the town. This, together with the loot taken from Porto Bello itself, meant that the daring exploit had yielded a vast treasure to be shared out.

"And now, Señor," said the Spanish officer after the ransom of the town had been agreed upon, "I have a message for you from the Governor of Panama. He asks you to be good enough to send him a specimen of the ordnance with which you were able to capture Porto Bello, a town we believed to be impregnable."

With twinkling eyes, Morgan drew a pistol from his belt and handed it to the surprised officer.

"There, Señor, send that to your Governor. There you have the only ordnance we used in the capture of Porto Bello. Inside the breech you will find the cannon balls we used. And you may add this, Señor, and I can assure you that I never spoke more seriously in my life. If the Governor of Panama will be good enough to keep this weapon for a twelvemonth, I and my buccaneers will call upon him in person to reclaim it!"

CHAPTER VIII

POLLY FLINDERS APPEARS

LOADED with loot, our vessels entered Port Royal Harbour again. News had already been sent to Jamaica reporting the capture of Porto Bello. Admiral Morgan rather expected Sir Thomas Modyford to pay him an immediate visit of congratulation. In this he was disappointed. Instead there came an officer from shore bearing a missive for the Admiral.

Morgan read it, and as he did so a dark scowl overspread his face.

"Does he think we buccaneers are a lot of slaves?" he shouted angrily, and flung the Governor's message to the deck. "Tell Sir Modyford," he continued, "that I will endeavour to wait on him to-morrow. For the present I am too fatigued, having just returned from an action that had not been without benefit to England."

As the officer descended into his boat, the Admiral turned to Captain Knocker and explained what had caused his ire. "He orders me to wait on him at once as though I'm one of the officers under his command instead of one of the Brotherhood. Blood and bones, but he'll find the buccaneer fleet can get along without him if needs be, though I'm willing to fight on England's side so long as the pay is good."

Algy, meanwhile, had been gazing towards the land with longing in his eyes. He had grown much manlier during his sojourn with the buccaneers, though he still provided a constant target for their jests and witticisms. His health was undoubtedly better, and his appetite so improved that he would eat food that before his abduction would have nauseated him by its very appearance. Yet he longed to feel dry land under his feet again, and to find himself amongst civilised people. He was no more at home amid the rough, uncouth buccaneers than a kitten surrounded by a host of porcupines.

"Won't you return with me, Arthur?" he asked me plaintively that evening. "I am sure Sir Thomas would forgive your escapade. Let us steal ashore to-night."

Big Dixon heard his remark, and asked him how he proposed going ashore. My old tutor replied, with a certain amount of pride, that he could swim there with ease, though I am sure he would have drowned long before reaching the shore.

"And what about Master Jack?" asked Big Dixon.

"Master Jack? Who's Master Jack?" queried the puzzled Algy.

"Master Jack Shark. You'd make a dainty supper for him, I'll be bound."

After that Algy would have tried to escape by swimming only at the point of a pistol. Yet he had quite set his mind on escaping, and wanted me to help him steal one of the boats.

"Not I, Algy," I said. "You know well enough why I ran away. 'Twas to learn news of my father, and to rescue him if it were possible. So long as the buccaneers are likely to be of service to me in my purpose, so long shall I remain with them."

Algy ceased trying to persuade me after a while, but himself had no stomach for another voyage in Morgan's vessel. So, finding I was resolved to remain, he began to beseech my aid in getting the Admiral to consent to him being put ashore.

"He'll do it for you, Arthur," he pleaded, "and remember it was through you I was abducted."

The poor man's misery did not leave me unmoved, yet I feared that directly he set foot upon land he would hasten to Sir Thomas Modyford. Therefore, before promising my help, I resolved that Algy must first guarantee not to betray my whereabouts to the Governor.

"But suppose the Admiral refuses," sighed Algy mournfully. "That would mean another voyage amongst these—these——" and words failed him.

"He'll let you go right enough," I told him cheerily. "But if he won't, don't be down in the dumps. I'll help you lower the jolly-boat one night, and you can row yourself ashore, with nobody the wiser."

It was a pity, as it turned out, that I put this idea into Algy's head, for when I came on deck in the morning, rubbing sleep-dimmed eyes, there was Big Dixon awaiting me with alarming news. Algy had disappeared, and a boat was missing! I was doubly alarmed; alarmed lest Algy, in his attempt to escape, might have met with some disaster; alarmed lest my whereabouts should be disclosed to Sir Thomas if Algy had safely reached the shore.

I was kept on tenterhooks until just before noon, when the look-out reported the Governor's boat putting off from shore. Morgan bade me fetch out and dust his best uniform (he was somewhat of a dandy upon occasions), and while he donned it, ordered me to fetch wine and fruit. Hastily I did so, being anxious to have finished my tasks before the Governor stepped upon the deck. And when the Admiral would have sent me upon another errand, I begged him to excuse me.

"Why, how's this?" he asked, scowling.

"Because, sir, I don't wish the Governor to know I'm on your ship. He may try to persuade you to send me back."

His scowl gave way to a loud laugh.

"Blood and bones, boy, but I forgot you'd run away from the Governor. I'll warrant he's got a rod in pickle, and that you'll smart for it when he lays hands upon you again. But don't worry that I'll give you away, lad. Here, slip behind this curtain. This will be the last place in which Sir Thomas will expect to find you."

Quickly I did as he suggested. Before I had been hidden many minutes one of the men came down with the message that the Governor wished to see the Admiral.

"Send him down!" ordered Morgan, and stood, arms crossed behind him, waiting for Sir Thomas Modyford's appearance.

"Good morning, sir," quoth the Admiral, as the Governor entered, and the door was pulled to behind him.

Sir Thomas uttered a curt good morning, and put his hat and cane upon the table before making any further remark.

"I sent a message yesterday to you to wait upon me," he said at length, in no pleasant voice.

"And I sent a reply that I was too tired. I presume you heard of our success in taking Porto

Bello? Such an expedition gives its commander but scant chance of repose."

"That is what I wanted to see you about. Who gave you orders to attack Porto Bello? Your commission, sir, relates only to the seizure of Spanish vessels plying in these waters."

Morgan flushed a deep red, and I saw his great hands clench and unclench behind him.

"Is that your gratitude?" he asked angrily. "Wasn't it from Porto Bello that danger threatened Jamaica itself? 'Tis reward, not blame, you should be giving me."

"Well, let that be," said the Governor, who looked every whit as angry as Morgan, though his voice remained calm and controlled. "I hear you have captured great store of loot at Porto Bello, to say nothing of a vast ransom for withdrawing your men."

"Well, sir, what of it?"

"Only that I should be pleased to learn what portion of it you intend handing to me on behalf of the King and Government of England?"

"Why, sir," said Morgan, "as to that I refer you to that self-same commission you mentioned some moments back. There it distinctly states that to recompense us of the Brotherhood for our services, all loot taken by us from the Spaniards shall be divided among us."

"Loot, perhaps, but it says nothing of a ransom."

"I'll not argue," retorted Morgan, "but set your mind at rest. Your Government won't see the colour of the money. And for why? 'Tis already shared out among my men, and to get back money from buccaneers—save in the rum-shops—is far less healthy than trying to drive off a hungry lion from its kill."

Sir Thomas Modyford bit his lips, and controlled his anger as best he could. Morgan, however, was aroused, and as is often the way with violent men, wanted the quarrel to continue.

"And pray what is your next complaint?" he asked. "Having done England good service by capturing Porto Bello with scant four hundred men, naturally I expect a number of complaints to be levelled at my head."

"Well, Admiral Morgan, if you must have it, there is another complaint. And as I have a witness in the case, perhaps you will allow his presence."

"By all means," replied Morgan, with exaggerated politeness. Whereupon the Governor stepped to the door and opened it to usher in—Algy.

Algy was no longer the unkempt, unshaven fellow he had been as a buccaneer. He had donned fresh clothes, his hair was well groomed and his beard shaven. For all that there remained traces of his recent voyage in the brighter glow of his eyes, the fresher, healthier hue of his cheeks.

"Well!" roared Morgan, fixing his eyes upon Algy as though he meant to petrify him with a glance, "what have *you* to say against me, eh?"

Whether it was because his recent experiences had stiffened his manhood or because the Governor's presence gave him confidence, Algy did not quail before that fierce glance.

"Sir," said he, "the only thing I have to complain about is that you have the boy, Arthur Ellis, upon your ship."

"And what about your own abduction? Have

you no complaint to make of that?" asked the Governor, surprised into raising his voice.

"No, sir. So long as Arthur is given back, I have nothing to say concerning my own voyage," responded Algy.

In that moment my respect for my former tutor leaped up high. Truly I had not imagined he had such an interest in my welfare. Feeling it was my business to show pluck likewise, I stepped forth from my place of concealment, and confronted the angry Governor.

"So you are here, are you?" he cried, and his hand stretched forth to his cane.

"Yes, sir, and the reason was given to you in the note left behind me, though I did not tell you I intended joining Admiral Morgan's fleet. Please don't think me ungrateful, but I could not remain quietly with you without knowing whether my father was killed or a prisoner."

Admiral Morgan's own wrath disappeared in face of my distress.

"Don't be too hard on the boy, Sir Thomas," said he. "If you had seen the way he fought, as bravely as a full-grown man, you'd be proud of him, stick me if you wouldn't."

Even Algy had a word to say in my favour.

"It will interest you, Sir Thomas, to know that Arthur's efforts have not been unsuccessful. From one of the Spanish prisoners he has learned that Sir Hugh Ellis is alive, but in Spanish hands, either at Maracaybo or Panama."

It would take too long to describe the rest of that stormy meeting, which did not finish till a full hour later. At first nothing would suit the Governor except that I should be taken back straightway to his house, there to receive a sound caning. With Morgan and Algy to back me up, however, the caning was dropped out of the programme. Then a compromise was reached, by which I was to live with the Governor while the fleet was in harbour, but if it embarked on any voyage likely to bring news of, or bearing help to, my father, I was to be allowed to join Morgan's own ship. The final promise wrung from the Governor was what chiefly pleased me. It was no less than this: that he would send Admiral Morgan in command of an expedition to Maracaybo Lagoon as soon as the fleet could be re-equipped.

"And now," said Admiral Morgan, when all these items had been concluded, to my great satisfaction at least, "to show there's no ill-feeling left behind, let us crack a bottle together. I'll promise you wine as fine as ever you've tasted. 'Tis the pick of the Governor's cellar at Porto Bello."

Whereupon the four of us sat down, feeling as affectionate towards one another as though Morgan and the Governor had never had words, as though I had never run away from Sir Thomas's house, and as though Algy had never had the unpleasant experience of being kidnapped by the buccaneers. Nor was Harry Morgan's promise of a splendid wine unfulfilled. It was as sweet and smooth to the palate as ever I had drunk before, and in its rich flavour were washed away all remnants of the discord that had lately existed between us.

There followed weary days in Port Royal, with little prospects (so far as I could see) of the Governor's promise to send an expedition to Maracaybo being fulfilled. Meanwhile the buccaneers were enjoying their rest in harbour. Thanks to their share of the Porto Bello loot, most of them had money to burn. It was a case with them of, "Eat and drink while you may. To-morrow, as like as not, you'll be killed. And if you aren't, there's plenty more loot to be got for the asking."

One incident occurred during my stay with the Governor which gave me fresh news of my father. Big Dixon, who was in the habit of calling upon me each evening, in company with Fiddler Jim, turned up one night with a short, squat, dark-skinned man. At first I did not recognise the fellow, but when Dick mentioned that he had been aboard the *Rover* I was all agog to hear his story.

"Do you mind me now, young sir?" he asked, holding out a great, dirty paw for me to shake. "Polly Flinders they called me, though I reckon I'm not much like a lass to look at, now am I?"

In all honesty I could not say he was, but changed the subject by asking him how he had come to escape when the *Rover* was taken.

"Escaped, say you? Ay, 'twas most unlikely to my mind that any of us would escape when two Spanish galleons laid us aboard. Up came the Dons in their scores, an' we turned back to back to fight 'em, well knowing we could never beat 'em off. But your father, an' Cap'n Barrett, set us such an example that for a long time not one of us would have been craven enough to throw down his arms.

"We were so outnumbered that it was a wonder we weren't swept over the side by their first rush. Cap'n Barrett brought two of them down with his pistols, then set about him, right royally, with a cutlass. Your father, young sir, for all that he looked pale and worried, fought with his sword as coolly as though he were fightin' with another gentleman, for practice-like, with buttons on their sword points. More than one he hurt, till a bullet in the arm made him change his sword to his left hand."

"Was he wounded badly?" I asked, trembling at the thought of the perils he must have braved in that affair.

"Not badly, young master. When last I saw your father he was well, his wounds nearly healed, and himself in no danger. Well, to get back to the fight. Seein' that half our men were down, an' the rest weary of the fight, the Cap'n knew that it would not be long before the *Rover* would be in Spanish hands. That he could not bear. I heard him whisper to Sir Hugh Ellis, 'Hold 'em in play for another five minutes, an' I'll blow up the ship.' Your father nodded cheerily, but I can tell you my knees shook beneath me. 'Tis no pleasant feeling to know that any moment you might be blown sky-high. Anyways, I said and did nothing, but fought on, hopin' that death would soon come to save me from that blowin'-up. 'Better a pike-thrust or a pistol ball,' thought I, 'than to be blown into bits.'"

"Don't seem to make much manner of difference to me," objected Big Dixon. "If you were dead you'd be blown up, just the same."

Polly Flinders scratched his head ruminatively. "Why, you're in the right of it, Dick," he admitted regretfully. "Anyways, alive nor dead, I wasn't blown up. And for why? Because before he could leave the deck, a musket-ball struck him in the back, killing him."

"May the Lord rest his soul!" said Big Dixon, deeply moved, for Captain Barrett was a fine skipper, respected and admired by every man that had sailed under him.

"Amen," added Flinders. "Well, maties, the

sight of our Captain bein' shot down made us forget our own danger for a while. We just went mad, an' had there been a few more of us, we might have driven the Dons back to their own ships. But more of us fell, an' when your father, who had kept all along in the very thick of the fight, received a blow upon the head that stretched him senseless, the rest of us threw down our arms.

"Give the Dons their due, they were merciful to us. Your father they tended, soon bringing him back to consciousness. Cap'n Barrett they buried like a true sailor into the deep, an' those of us as were wounded had our hurts cared for. 'Twas only when they landed us at Porto Bello that our real troubles started."

With that, Polly Flinders shuddered, and a look of stark fear came into his eyes.

"Tell me," said I, though I dreaded to hear the horrors he appeared to have to tell. And in his uncouth, sailor fashion he told me. How one by one they had been visited by an officer of the Inquisition, and questioned concerning his religious faith, and since one and all professed the truths taught in England, had been dubbed 'heretic' and threatened with torture and the stake. I shall never forget the horror I experienced when Polly withdrew his left hand, which he had held all this time in his shirt front, and offered it for my inspection. The thumb was mangled beyond description, and beyond hope of cure. "The thumb-screw," he said bitterly. "They reckon by treating the body cruelly to save the soul. May their bodies and souls alike rot for everlastin', the devils!"

"Was my—was my father treated like this?" I managed to blurt out.

"No, young sir, I'm glad to say, though as to what will happen to him, 'tis in God's hands. By reason of his wound and the blow upon his head, he was reckoned unfit to endure the torture. By the time 'e was almost better, news came that Porto Bello was goin' to be attacked, an' all prisoners were sent off, some to Panama and some to Maracaybo."

"Were you all kept together, that you know how my father fared?"

"Not whilst we were in Porto Bello, young master. But not all the Dons were cruel to us ashore. There was a youth, a pale, sickly sort of lad, that had a heart of gold. Time and again, when we were flung back in our cells, almost mad with pain after an hour at the hands of our torturers, he would creep in with salves for our hurts, and comfortin' words. 'Twas he that gave me news how your father, an' my comrades, were farin'."

How pleased I was that I had been able to lead to safety the Spanish youth I had encountered at Porto Bello! I felt certain that he had been the Good Samaritan who had, at great risk, carried comfort and healing to the poor unfortunate English prisoners in his charge.

"When the orders came that we were to be moved," went on Polly Flinders, "I was near to goin' mad with joy. Anything looked better to me than remainin' where I was, to be gradually crushed into bits by their devilish engines. One day, close about noon, we were led from our cells into the open, and how our eyes blinked in the strong sunlight! We would have fallen into one another's arms, so good was it to see friendly faces again, but the Spanish soldiers drove us apart with their pikes. We were then chained together like slaves (as, indeed, we were), and at last came the order to move. Did I say we were glad to be out of our cells? It wasn't long before we changed our views on that. None of us had boots on our feet, none of us had cover for back or head to guard us from the fierce heat. There were stones below to bruise our feet, the sun above to blister our backs, the heat to make our tongues parched, yet no water to ease our thirst. An' if one of us should stumble, or if our pace wasn't fast enough, there were drivers who walked up an' down the line, and lashed us, like so many cattle, an' us not able to defend ourselves."

Anger nearly choked me as I listened, and there and then I vowed vengeance upon my father's persecutors if ever I could identify them.

"Ay," continued Polly, "at times I think it was all a frightful nightmare, till the sores upon my back smart shrewdly to remind me 'twas cruel fact I am telling ye of. Pedro the Hairy was the cruellest to us. He's a giant in size, bigger than you, Dick, and his great body is covered thickly with dark hairs. Black he is to look at, but blacker the cruel heart that beats within him."

"Pedro the Hairy! I'll remember the name. Did he——?" I could not finish the question. I wanted to say, "Did he ever ill-treat my father?"

"I was goin' to tell you, boy, though 'twill hurt you in the tellin'. It was at the end of the second day. We had marched perhaps a score of miles, an' we were no longer awake as we walked. We merely dragged one foot after the other, an' longed for death. 'Twas then I stumbled, an' could not scramble to my feet again. Pedro the Hairy came cursing roundly, his cruel whip in hand. Once!

Twice! Thrice! It whistled across my bare back as though the lash would cut me right through. Then I remember a body fallin' across mine, and again the whistle of the lash. But it did not fall upon me. Do you know what had happened, boy? Your father—bless him for the noble gentleman he is—had flung himself upon me to protect me, bein' the next one to me in the line—an' received upon his body the rest of the lashes meant for me.

"I must have fainted, and when I came to again, young master, it was night, an' the moon shinin' above. Presently I remembered what must have happened, and dragged myself alongside your father. He was lyin' on the ground, an' his back —Heaven above, I dare not tell you the state of it. I began to thank him, but he would not let me say a word. An' somehow or other, in spite of his sufferin', he managed to smile, an' gripped me by the hand an' bade me be of good courage. Boy, you've a father that any lad might be proud to own, an' if you don't do all you can to save him, you're not worthy of him."

"Polly," said I earnestly, "either I rescue him, if he still lives, or perish in the effort. And as for that brute, Pedro the Hairy, if ever Fate throws him in my path, I'll do my utmost to repay him for his cruelty."

"Ay!" chimed in Big Dixon, "an' here's another of the same mind. Let me once get my hands about that hairy fellow's neck——"

He did not finish his sentence in words, but the way he tensed his muscles and curled his strong fingers was far more eloquent than mere speech.

"I knew the youngster would be a chip o' the old block," quoth Polly approvingly. "What's more, I'm one who'll join ye when you set out in search o' him. Well, my lads, you'll be wonderin' how I managed to escape. Just luck, that's all. The chains that bound me to your father must have had a flaw in them. One night, as we lay restin', I woke up to find your father workin' away, as cautious as he might, at breakin' the chains that j'ined us. I could do nothin' to help him, the flaw in the fetter being too close to my back. Hour after hour—or so it seemed to me—he worked patiently away, filing at the chain with a rough piece of stone he had found. At times, when a sentry drew near, he had to stop, an' we both lay down, quakin' inwardly lest we 'ad been observed. But at last the job was done; the chain was broken, an' I, once the first men o' the file o' slaves, was no longer chained to any one.

"My first thought was to make off as fast as I could. Yet I stopped myself in time, though my heart was pumpin' with fear all the while in case one of the guards should find out I was free. But your father, young sir, told me I could do nothin' by stayin'. The dawn was near at hand, an' if I waited longer it would only mean bein' chained up again with the rest. Even as it was, I should have little enough time to get clear of the camp before my escape was discovered, an' it was certain that parties would be sent out to recapture me.

"So, pressin' his hand and thankin' him for what he'd done, I set off. But there, you won't want to hear the rest of my adventures, an' how, at length, I was able to steal a canoe, an' how I was picked up by the *Oxford* frigate, one o' the buccaneers' ships. You'll be anxious to hear the message sent you by your father."

"By my father?" cried I, all excitement. "Did he send me a message?"

"When he bid me good-bye, he whispered this to me, 'If you escape, Polly, try to find out whether my boy reached shore in safety. Seek him out, an' tell him I am well, an' far from despairin', that the Dons are either takin' me to Maracaybo or to Panama. If he wants to attempt my rescue, he may, but what I pray for above all else is his own safety, an' that the Lord will watch over him.'"

CHAPTER IX

WE REACH MARACAYBO

IMPATIENT though I was to be off in search of my father, nothing could be done until Morgan's fleet was ready to sail. It was not until the following year, January 1669 to be precise, that the Admiral sent word to all the buccaneers in the Spanish Main who wished to join him in an enterprise promising (as he said) "no little danger, fighting, and booty," to assemble forthwith at a rendezvous upon Cow Island.

By this time, such was the name Morgan had won for his daring and success, that buccaneers of all nationalities flocked to the rendezvous.

Camp was formed upon land, and while Morgan, with Knocker as chief adviser, had in front of him all the volunteers for his expedition, allotting those he adjudged fit to various commands, he sent his captains to ravage the Spanish settlements along the Cuban coast, not so much in the hope of winning gold and silver, as to obtain provisions for his fleet.

My own desire was to accompy Captain Gentle upon one of these trips, in the hope of hearing further news concerning my father's fate. The Admiral, however, kept me at his side, promising that I might join in the main fighting, when it should happen, but adding that he had vowed to Sir Thomas Modyford not to let me run into unnecessary danger. But though I had no great objection to remaining with Morgan, it was most galling to see the way in which Knocker influenced him, often in evil courses.

It was Knocker who led to the treachery practised upon the French ship in the bay. Morgan had tried hard to persuade the captain of this ship—a fine vessel, mounting twenty-four iron and twelve brass guns—to join his command. The Frenchman, a friend of Pierre, who had left Morgan on the eve of the Porto Bello attack, would have none of it.

"Why not invite the French officers aboard?" suggested Knocker, with a significant wink.

"You mean——?" asked Morgan, only dimly comprehending.

"Invite 'em aboard. Clap the hatches on them. Seize their vessel! 'Tis easy enough, on my soul."

"But what will the French buccaneers say? It may cause a split in my force again."

"Never fear that! After what you did at Porto Bello, the Frenchmen will follow you. What care they what happens to their officers? Why, most of the Frenchmen aboard yon vessel would give their eyes to join with you."

So Knocker had his way. Invitations were issued to the French officers to dine upon the *Oxford* frigate, Morgan's flagship, and they, suspecting no evil, came aboard.

The dinner began well, and the Frenchmen were in high spirits. So was Morgan, but from a different cause. After the meal had ended, the Admiral called for the glasses to be filled, before rising in his place, with brimming goblet uplifted.

"Brethren of the Coast!" he began, and his eyes twinkled with fun the while, "here's success to my new enterprise, and may your vessel bear a noble part therein." And while the amazed guests looked from one to the other, wondering what might be the meaning of his strange words, the door of the cabin was flung open, and four buccaneers pointed muskets at the Frenchmen. Simultaneously Admiral Morgan, Knocker, and the other English officers whipped out their pistols, so that all the guests were covered.

"Mais, monsieur, what is ze meaning of zis?" asked the French skipper, appealingly, of Morgan.

"Ze meaning of zis," explained Morgan, imitating the English of his prisoner, "is zat we require ze use of your vessel."

"Ay!" cried Knocker, with a great laugh. "The flies having walked into the spider's web, must remain there. March 'em away forward, lads!"

Resistance would have meant death, and the indignant Frenchmen, at the point of the musket, were forced to proceed forward, where they were clapped under hatches. Meanwhile boats were put off from our sides, full of buccaneers armed to the teeth. The *Oxford's* guns were trained upon the French vessel. However, no fighting ensued. Not only was there no officer left aboard to organise any resistance, but the Frenchmen had no suspicion of anything being wrong, the greater part of them, in fact, being ashore. The English buccaneers took possession of the vessel without a shot being fired, the remaining Frenchmen being sent to join their officers aboard the *Oxford* until such time as Morgan could give them an opportunity to join his expedition.

Morgan and Knocker were mightily elated at the success of their stratagem. They ordered me to bring more wine aft, and sent a butt of rum forward for the men to broach in celebration of the occasion.

Very soon there came floating to our ears uproarious shouts of mirth, and then a loud call for Fiddler Jim. Presently the merry strains of his fiddle could he heard, mingled with the shouts and singing of the men, followed by the shuffling of many feet upon the deck as the fiddle changed into a dance tune.

The officers had been drinking no less heavily than the men. Morgan was growing red in the face, and swaying uncertainly upon his feet. Knocker remained seated, while he drank glass after glass of wine in rapid succession, and to me his face appeared to leer more evilly at me with every mouthful he took. The other officers, each in his own way, gave signs of being intoxicated.

"Why should they have music forward, an' we aft drink without?" demanded Knocker, in a thick voice.

"Boy," said Morgan, turning to me and gazing at me with bleary eyes. "Run along forrard, an' tell Fiddler Jim to come here at once. Hurry, now!"

I made my way forward as fast as I could, and found that the drink which had been so freely shared out amongst the men was already having its effect. Many lay about in drunken slumber, others lounged about, trying to drink, but spilling more liquor over their clothes than down their throats. Just a few still made clumsy efforts to dance in time to the merry tune Jim was fiddling.

The only sober men I could see, apart from Fiddler Jim, were my friends, Big Dixon and Polly Flinders. Loyal hearts! They did not drink with the others because, night or day, they intended to be ready to help me if their aid should be required.

I gave Fiddler Jim the Admiral's message, and, in spite of the drunken remonstrance of some of the dancers, he prepared to follow me. Whereupon one of the fellows pulled forth his knife and threatened to stick Jim if he did not again start his playing.

Fiddler Jim stood uncertain, being, as a rule, slow to quarrel, whereat the fellow flourished his knife menacingly, slightly wounding my cheek with the movement. That was enough for Big Dixon. In two bounds he was at my side, and a swift upper-cut of his big, right fist had lifted the buccaneer clear of the deck.

In a trice Polly Flinders had joined his mate, and the pair, with fists clenched ready for action, glared round them to see if any other dared offer violence. Finding none to harm us, Fiddler Jim and I, with our escort, made our way aft.

I was on the point of leading the way down to the cabin when there came a mighty flash of flame and a terrific explosion that lifted me clean off my feet and flung me against the rail.

It was several minutes before my dazed senses recovered. When at length I struggled to my feet, I found the fore part of the frigate practically blown away and what was left burning fiercely. Blackened timbers strewed the sea, and fragments were still descending about our ears.

"Are you all right?" roared Big Dixon, memory of the explosion causing him to shout.

"All right but for a few bruises. What has happened?"

"I reckon those Frenchies have had their revenge. They've blown up the *Oxford* and themselves with it. We're sinking fast. Best lower a boat, if there's one left!"

"I'm going to look for Morgan," I answered, and led the way. Big Dixon, after yelling to Fiddler

Jim and Polly to lower a boat, came lumbering after me.

The door of Morgan's cabin had been flung off its hinges, and lay jammed across the doorway. There was no sign of life within. Big Dixon drew back a few yards, heaved forward his shoulder aggressively, and charged at the door. It gave way before him, and I followed him into the cabin.

Morgan, Knocker, and the rest were sprawled out in various attitudes. At first I thought they were dead, but on listening at Morgan's chest heard his heart beating strongly.

Big Dixon stooped to pick up the Admiral. I tried to carry one of the others, but my strength was insufficient, so I followed my comrade to the deck.

"She'll be sinking soon," cried Dixon, over his shoulder. "I hope they've a boat ready for us."

They had not, every boat having been smashed to atoms: there was no danger of drowning, however, for others were near at hand from ships in the bay.

Big Dixon lowered the Admiral's body and cast a calculating eye at the fire raging in what remained of the fore part of the frigate.

"We've a few more minutes to spare," said he. "Keep with the Admiral, Arthur. Now, lads, follow me, and we'll bring up the others."

While my companions were below, I did what I could to revive the Admiral, but though I bathed his face with water, he remained unconscious. By the time three more of the officers had been brought on deck, two boats had been run alongside and some of the buccaneers had scrambled aboard. These lowered the unconscious bodies into the boats, while Big Dixon and his comrades once more descended to the cabin on their work of rescue.

"That's the lot," said Big Dixon presently, laying down the man he was carrying.

I looked at the man's face. "He's not the last," said I. "Where's Knocker?"

A hard look settled upon Dixon's face.

"I've a notion," said he, "that it would be a mighty fine thing for us—to say nothing of Morgan—if we left that rat to be drowned. He bears no goodwill to us, nor to the Admiral either. I've heard him trying to stir up the men against Morgan, tellin' them they don't get a fair share of the loot."

Much as I detested Knocker, I could not agree to leaving him to be drowned like a rat in a trap. Very reluctantly Big Dixon followed me when I dived below, and with ungentle grasp carried Morgan's treacherous confidant to safety.

"I hope you'll not regret it, lad," said he, as he handed down his burden to the men in the boat below.

A quick search was made through what was left of the *Oxford* to see if there were any other survivors. There was none. All the French, officers and men, had perished in the explosion of their own making, and apart from the few of us who had been aft, none of the English had escaped.

When Morgan came to himself and learned what had happened to his frigate, he bit his teeth in his vexation. But he was of too dauntless a disposition to have his plans thwarted by an accident of this kind, however severe a blow to his already weak forces. He sent a message to the captains to come aboard his vessel, and when they arrived bluntly announced his intention of attacking Maracaybo!

"Are you asking for our views?" asked a quiet-voiced man, small of stature, but renowned as one of the craftiest and most daring of the Brethren of the Coast. He was known as Musket Jack, for whenever he led a boarding-party, he fought, holding a musket by the barrel, using it as a club. I had noticed him particularly of late, for he had been often in the company of Knocker, who, I suspected later, had done much to persuade him to oppose Morgan's plans.

"Am I asking for views? If any of you can suggest any stratagem for taking Maracaybo fort, I am. If it's to try to dissuade me from making the attempt, I should advise such a one to save his breath."

"Nevertheless, Admiral, I will say my say, first pointing out that your fleet is not so strong that you can afford to have any captains refusing to sail with you."

Morgan swallowed this open threat with an obvious effort. Seeing the Admiral said nothing against him proceeding, Musket Jack leaned back in his chair, and spread open hands across his chest, finger-tips lightly resting together.

"You say you intend leading your force against Maracaybo. You know what that means. There's a fort commanding the entrance to a lake, which must first be captured. You have too few men to leave a garrison, while we're in the lake sacking Maracaybo, and perhaps Gibraltar. By the time we're ready to sail out, what's to prevent the Dons having remanned the fort, so that their guns command the passage through which we have to pass?"

The quiet words of Musket Jack made quite an impression upon the captains present.

Morgan, however, blustering mightily, hastened to reply.

"What if they do? If we can take the fort once, we can take it twice. We'll dismantle the fort as we sail in, so that it will take weeks to fortify it again."

"Maybe, Admiral," went on Musket Jack, "but remember you may be weeks in the lake. And when you come to leave, there may be more than the fort to contend with. There may be Spanish galleons waiting to dispute the passage."

"And if there are," quoth Morgan, with a sneer. "Haven't we ever fought and beaten galleons before? The sight of a four-decker makes my blood tingle at the prospect of a fresh prize."

"Apart from the French vessel you have managed to obtain," continued Musket Jack, "and my own ship—which I don't intend to be sailed into a trap—your largest vessel only mounts fourteen guns, and those but small ones."

"If my largest vessel mounted only pistols, I'd still go," cried Morgan, smiting his fist upon the table, being unable longer to control his temper, "and hang any coward that refuses to sail with me! Let me see 'em now, so that I know who will follow me."

"My name is too well known to the Brethren for any to account me coward for refusing to follow you," replied Musket Jack, raising his voice not a whit because of the Admiral's bluster. "I call upon every captain here who doesn't wish to lose his ship to follow my example. Better sail away, and be dubbed a coward, say I, than remain, and have to act like a fool."

With that he rose, and quitted the cabin, and notwithstanding the fierce gleam in Morgan's eyes, several others followed his example. It was specially noticeable that most of the Frenchmen left, it being freely rumoured that they were very bitter concerning the seizure of the French ship on the previous day, which had resulted in the loss of so many of their countrymen.

"Well, we're better rid of such scum," cried Morgan, doing his best to sound cheerful. "Always remember, the fewer there are of us, the more the booty."

He then gave orders to the captains still loyal to him to reckon up the number of men remaining. As Musket Jack had said, his largest vessel, apart from the French ship, mounted but fourteen small guns. He had seven others, and barely five hundred men, instead of the thousand he had expected. Nevertheless, to my great joy, Morgan had no intention of abandoning the expedition. How I prayed, as the little fleet weighed anchor, that this adventure might lead me to my father, and secure his release!

Two days later found us within sight of Maracaybo fort, which commanded the entrance to the great inlet beyond. Scorning concealment, Morgan steered his ship full in face of the fort, enduring its fire with such fortitude as he could until near enough to use his own small guns. The rest of the fleet followed him right gallantly. And now was found the benefit of the regular gun-drill which Morgan had insisted upon the buccaneers practising ever since he first held his rendezvous at Cow Island. Each gun was cleaned, loaded, laid and fired with beautiful speed and accuracy. While few of the defenders' shots fell aboard us (so skilfully did Captain Knocker manœuvre his vessel) there was hardly a round from the buccaneers' guns which did not fall upon the fortress.

Yet if Morgan had hoped to win the fortress with but little expenditure of ammunition, he found himself sadly mistaken. At dawn our bombardment had commenced. At noon we were still firing with such guns as were cool enough, while the fortress continued to reply stoutly, if not quite so heavily as at first. Hour after hour the gun duel continued, the while Morgan fumed and fretted upon the quarter-deck, not daring to order an attack in the boats because of the scarcity of his men, and the fear that many of the boats would be smashed because of the cannonade from the fort.

Not till the sun was close to dropping from sight did the fire from the fort really slacken. Then it suddenly ceased. Though half fearing a ruse, Morgan determined to risk an assault in the boats before nightfall. He himself took his place in the leading boat, myself with him, and with twenty others behind, each crammed with men armed to the teeth, we set out for the now silent fort.

The rowers bent sturdily to their oars, expecting every moment that the guns of the fort would re-commence their cannonade. Yet not a shot was fired. Unopposed, the boats grounded in shallow water, and with muskets held high above their heads the buccaneers waded ashore and ran towards the fort.

The garrison had retreated—that was plain. Not a single musket-shot greeted our approach. We clambered our way into the defences, finding everywhere proof of the accuracy of our fire. There were many breaches in the walls. Here a gun was smashed from touch-hole to muzzle; there a little group of slain lay sprawled about a hole which showed where the fatal shot had fallen.

The buccaneers, true to their instincts when fighting was over, ran hither and thither in search of anything of value. I had other plans. With Big Dixon, Fiddler Jim, and Polly Flinders to help me, I began a search for any wounded Spaniards who might be able to give me more news of my father.

At first it seemed as though the garrison, on its withdrawal, had carried all the wounded away to safety. It was Polly who found a wounded Don, pale as death, in one of the underground chambers. To our astonishment he had been gagged, and besides that, bound hand and foot so that he could neither move nor cry out for assistance. Not till later, from one of the garrison who afterwards fell into our hands, did I learn the true reason for this. The man, Alonso by name, had been terrified at the thought of being captured by the buccaneers and had attempted to flee long before the commander of the fort had given orders to evacuate. In punishment he had been tied to a post in an exposed position within the fortress, but though severely wounded during this ordeal, had received no fatal hurt. When, therefore, the time came for the fort to be abandoned, orders were given to hide the man below ground so that he might share the fate it was hoped the buccaneers would suffer.

All the time we were removing the gag from the man's throat, and loosening his bonds, I was struck by the terrible look of fear in his eyes. My first thought was that it was due to his terror at being in the hands of buccaneers, for tales of their terrible cruelty were well known upon the Spanish Main. When his gag was removed, he made strenuous and, at first, vain efforts to speak. Finding this unsuccessful, he made frantic gesticulations, while the frightened look in his eyes compelled attention.

"What does the old fool mean by wavin' his arms about in the air like that?" demanded Polly angrily.

"P'raps he's prayin'," hazarded Fiddler Jim. "He keeps pushin' up his hands heavenwards."

Meanwhile I had been watching him carefully, puzzling my head to find out his meaning. "I do believe he's trying to say we're going to be blown up," I cried at length, and turning to the man, I asked him, in his own language, if this were so.

"Si, Señor, si," he answered excitedly, my question apparently restoring to him the power of speech. "They've left a train burning which will blow up the magazine. Any moment—any moment——"

"Where? Quick!" I asked, but he could do nothing but wave his hand distractedly and repeat, "Any moment—any moment."

"Quick!" I cried to my comrades. "You, Dixon, tell Morgan, so that he can set his men to search. You others look for the powder magazine."

"Why not clear out?" suggested Polly. "'Twould be safest."

"And leave the others to be blown up? It's upon the buccaneers I depend to save my father. Quick now!"

It was I who found the flame licking its way towards where the powder was stored—found it in the nick of time when it had but another foot to travel before blowing us all sky-high. In frantic haste I flung myself upon it, beating it out with my clenched hands. And the danger over, reaction came. I fainted clean away.

Morgan was holding me in his arms when I came

to myself. Around us were grouped most of the buccaneers, gazing interestedly at me. I caught the tail-end of the Admiral's speech, "—just in time to save us all being blown to glory. Give the lad a cheer to let him know we're proud of him."

Deep-throated came the required cheer which thrilled me strangely. It was not easy to win the approbation of these brave but cruel men. Not satisfied with the cheer, one of their number stepped forward, and touched his forelock.

"Beg pardon, sir, but you know, as we all do, that 'tis the custom of the Brotherhood to make a gift to any one of us as does special service. With your leave, sir, I makes bold to propose as how we offer to this young lad his pick of the spoils of this expedition."

"Hear! hear!" growled many of the others, and none appeared to be opposed to the suggestion.

"I'm quite willin'," agreed Morgan. "What say you, lads? Shall we do as Roger here suggests?"

"Ay! ay!" came the hearty response, and I, having been put upon my feet again, glanced gratefully around. But as for loot, no desire for that crossed my mind. Impulsively I addressed the men.

"It's very fine of you to make me the offer you have done. I don't want money, however. What I want is your help—your help to release my father who is a prisoner of the Dons. He may be in Maracaybo, or maybe he's at Panama. If I don't find him here, how many of you will march across the isthmus in search of him?"

How well I remember that moonlight scene! How loudly still in my ears rings the echo of the hearty shouts that answered my question! Looking round upon their resolute faces, how could I feel anything but confident hope that my great desire would be accomplished?

Early next morning our forces set off overland for the settlement of Maracaybo. We were led by the Spaniard who had warned us of the plot to blow up the fort. Contrary to their usual custom, the buccaneers had neither tortured nor slain him. Indeed, he was so anxious to do anything to save himself from harm, that he was likely to be of great use as a guide while we remained in the lagoon.

As he led us by a narrow trail through the thick woods which ringed in Maracaybo, with Morgan's permission I talked to the man. Big Dixon, and my other comrades, stalked closely behind me, weapons held ready, for they feared an ambush. I myself was too excited to have any fears, for the guide had told me that some English prisoners had been sent to Maracaybo a month or so previously, but he believed that they had been transferred to Gibraltar, which lay farther along the inlet.

"Was there a tall man, square shoulders, blue eyes?" I questioned anxiously, and gave other details of my father's appearance.

Alonso shook his head gravely.

"It is hard, Señor, to distinguish one slave from another. Their skin becomes dark, their shoulders become bowed, their chins become bearded. But this I know, the English prisoners sent to Maracaybo were sailors captured from an English man-of-war last year. 'Tis rumoured that one of them was the Governor of Jamaica himself."

With this I had to be content. His last remark in particular raised my hopes. True my father was not the Governor of Jamaica, but rumour might easily exaggerate the importance of his office. Somehow I felt confident that I should find my father at Gibraltar.

We made our journey through the woods unmolested. Morgan spread out his men until they ringed the whole settlement. At a given signal we broke from cover, and ran as fast as we could towards the town.

There remained no one to oppose us. Men, women, children—even the animals—had fled in alarm at the news of our approach into the shelter of the woods around.

Nor was that the worst from the buccaneers' point of view. The inhabitants, in spite of their haste, had yet found time to take their treasures with them.

"Never mind, lads," shouted Knocker, indicating with a sweep of his cutlass the woods around. "We'll search them out, never fear. We'll burn, we'll use the rack, we'll put out eyes, my bully boys! There's treasure enough for all, my lads, if we only squeeze hard enough."

CHAPTER X

CAPTURED BY THE DONS

How the buccaneers scoured the woods around for the inhabitants of Maracaybo, and how they tortured their prisoners, old and young, demanding as the price of release from pain impossible ransoms, I do not propose to relate in detail.

For three weeks they remained in and about Maracaybo, searching for the vanished occupants, torturing those they found, and unearthing treasure when the hiding-place had been forced from unwilling lips. All the time I was in a fever of impatience to be off to Gibraltar, where perhaps my father lay a prisoner. I begged Morgan to lead his forces thither at once, but though I believe he was at first inclined to agree to my request, Knocker soon made him change his mind.

All Morgan would do was to send a message to the people of Gibraltar, by the hand of one of the Dons who had been tortured, who would serve as a warning, demanding the immediate surrender of all prisoners they held, together with a vast ransom, to be paid in pieces of eight, if they did not wish their settlement to be sacked.

Perhaps it was fortunate for my purpose that the people of Gibraltar sent back an insolent reply. News had reached us that a Spanish force, commanded by no less notable a leader than Don Alonso del Campo y Espinosa, had occupied the fort at the entrance to the Maracaybo Lagoon, and that the place was being put into a state of defence. Heavy guns were being mounted, and the garrison would be so strong (our spies informed us) that if we did not leave the lagoon at once, we might find our retreat cut off.

Knocker immediately called upon Morgan to set sail, claiming that the amount of loot to be taken at Gibraltar was not worth waiting for. Summoning all my courage, I ventured to oppose this advice in front of a full meeting of the captains of the expedition. Though I was somewhat of a favourite amongst them, they were, for the most part, inclined to vote for following the rogue's advice.

Before the matter could be decided, the prisoner who had borne Morgan's message to Gibraltar was conducted into our presence bearing an answer.

Morgan opened the missive handed to him, and as he read, his brow darkened.

"Listen, Brethren of the Coast," said he, "and when you have heard the insolent reply to our demands, then answer whether you will sail away without visiting Gibraltar.

> 'The inhabitants of Gibraltar do not pay ransom to cattle-slayers. They advise you to leave the lagoon of Maracaybo before the entrance is closed, and your retreat cut off for ever. If you want our prisoners, you must come and take them.'

Well, lads, you have heard their reply. Those who still vote for sailing away at once?"

Not a man, not even Knocker, raised his hand or voice.

"For paying a visit to Gibraltar? I thought so. We will hang up the writer of this message by his toes till the birds peck his eyes out. We start at noon."

A Spaniard named Diaz, whom we had found in the woods near Maracaybo, and who had betrayed many of his countrymen to us, was chosen as our guide to Gibraltar. Once more our passage was unopposed, and we found Gibraltar, despite the valiant message of its inhabitants, had been deserted. As at Maracaybo, the woods around were scoured for fugitives, and each one found was subjected to the most fearful tortures until he either divulged where his wealth was hidden or died under the torment.

As for my own party, we had no hand in the atrocities committed by the buccaneers. At Morgan's special order, we were allowed to question all prisoners before they were put on the rack or subjected to the other torments devised to wring from them their wealth.

The fourth prisoner we questioned had information to give us concerning the English slaves.

"They have been taken from Gibraltar," said he, "to a spot ten miles from here. It is well hidden and will of a certainty not be found by your men, since the path leading to it is known only to a very few."

"And do you know it?" I asked.

The man made no direct reply, but a crafty look came into his eyes.

"If I did, how would that benefit you—or me?"

To my shame I must confess that I made use of the tortures the buccaneers were wont to practise upon their captives to further my own plans.

"If you know where the prisoners are and lead us to them, you will escape some such fate as yonder compatriot of yours is suffering." And I pointed to where a Spaniard, stripped stark naked, had been spread out, face towards the ground, the whole weight of his body being supported by his thumbs and big toes, each of which was tied to a stake driven into the ground. To add to his torment, a large boulder had been placed upon the small of his back.

The Spaniard shuddered, and I knew he would be willing to do my will.

"Lead us to the English prisoners," said I, "and you shall be allowed to go free."

"Señor, it shall be as you desire," he promised.

I sent Fiddler Jim in search of Morgan to ask of him a force of buccaneers to accompany me to the hiding-place where the English slaves had been secreted. To my dismay, he returned with news that Morgan had set out with fifty men on some expedition and might be absent for several days.

In this dilemma, I sought Captain Gentle and asked him for aid.

"I'm sorry, lad, I can't lend you any men without Knocker's consent. The Admiral has left him in command."

"But will he help me? You know he has little liking for me."

"That I can't say, lad. But I'll come along with you and see if I can persuade him."

Together we approached Knocker, who looked at me with scornful eyes, though he greeted Gentle pleasantly enough. I told him what I wanted, emphasising the fact that Morgan had promised his aid in my search for my father, also that Sir Thomas Modyford had sent the expedition to

Maracaybo partly to win back the English prisoners.

Knocker heard me to the end, the while he gazed at me through half-closed eyes.

"Do your best to help the lad," pleaded Captain Gentle. "He's a plucky little devil."

"I'd like to help him," said Knocker slowly, and I could tell he was lying. "But I can't spare the men till the Admiral returns."

"The Dons will never dare to attack us, man!"

"D'you think they haven't spies, Cap'n Gentle? D'you think they don't know that Morgan and his fifty men have left us? D'you think if I allowed this lad another fifty, as he wants, that they'd not attack?"

"First time I knew Cap'n Knocker was so cautious," sneered Captain Gentle.

Knocker flushed at the insult, and started to his feet. Fearing lest the two captains should resort to arms, I hastened to avert the quarrel by asking Knocker if he would allow me and my friends to go in search of the prisoners if we took none of the buccaneers with us.

"Ay, you can put your own heads in a noose, if you like," he agreed, chuckling evilly. "I, for one, won't be worried if you find your father—and keep with him."

"The scoundrel," growled Captain Gentle, as we walked away. "He could spare you men enough if he chose. Why, the buccaneers are scattered all over the place, scouring the woods for Spaniards."

"I'll have to go alone, that's all," said I bitterly.

"I've a good mind to bring my own men," said Gentle, "but, like it or not, Knocker is in command. But remember this, boy, if you find it impossible to rescue your father without more help, send to me. I'll come then, though fifty men like yon scab order me back."

Big Dixon looked grave when I told him what had happened. "I'll come with you, right enough, Arthur," he said, "but it will be a risky business. I don't trust the rogue who is to be our guide. Likely enough he'll lead us into a trap."

"Ay," agreed Polly, "and I, for one, don't fancy falling into Spanish hands again."

"I must make the attempt," I said. "If my father is so near, as I believe, it would be too cowardly for words to fear attempting a rescue because we don't like our guide's face. And it's too risky to await Morgan's return. He may decide to beat his way out of the lagoon any day now."

"At any rate, wait till to-morrow," counselled Dixon. "Morgan may return before then, and give you the men you want. We'll start with the dawn, shall we?"

With this I agreed, and Polly and Fiddler Jim seemed satisfied also. We made full preparations for our hazardous trip. Muskets were cleaned and loaded, pistols freshly primed, and a supply of provisions packed. Big Dixon's load was twice as large as any of the others, and, when I tried to lift it, I found it almost beyond my powers.

I felt very uneasy that evening, as I sat close to the huge fire upon which a whole ox was roasting, and near which the buccaneers were sprawled at their ease. Perhaps it was Big Dixon's remarks, perhaps my own recognition of the dangers of our proposed expedition. Whatever the cause, I felt downright miserable, and all sorts of gloomy anticipations of coming disaster thronged my brain.

Not so my companions. Fiddler Jim was sitting upon a log, his violin tucked lovingly under his chin. And Big Dixon and Polly Flinders were singing a duet, the former with a deep bass voice, the latter in a sweet tenor:

> "They rove a noose in a hempen rope,
> They dropped it over his head, oh!
> They jerked him up in a hangdog dance
> Till Bobtail Dick was dead, oh!"

And then the listeners around joined in the chorus with more heartiness than unison.

> "So heave away, with a roundelay,
> (This be the song to sing, oh!)
> We're off to sea, and we leave the tree,
> Where Bobtail Dick doth swing, oh!"

The chorus haunted me in my dreams that night. Who the hero (or villain, more like) of the song was I had no idea. But it was a gloomy thought that a similar fate might be ours.

We breakfasted early, and set off before half the sun's rim had appeared above the sky-line. Big Dixon led the way, with the Spaniard beside him. He had tied a rope round the guide's waist, and the other end was fastened to his own belt. Before setting out he reminded the man that, at the first sign of treachery, he would be shot; but if he acted honestly by us, we would set him at liberty.

The light of a new day, and the warmth of the rising sun, put fresh heart into me. All around the wild life of the woods was already astir, and the chorusing of the birds awoke a fresh spring of hope within me. As I watched the tall figure of Big Dixon, swinging easily along, and gazed at the resolute faces of Fiddler Jim and Polly, I began to whistle from very lightheartedness, till I remembered that before our journey was over, caution might be necessary.

At first our way was easy. Once or twice we heard noises in the woods on either hand, and divined that we had alarmed some of the inhabitants of Gibraltar who were in hiding till the buccaneers had gone. But no one opposed our passage, and presently we found the path we were following had disappeared, and we were forced to slacken our pace as we pushed, and, at times, hacked, our way through the undergrowth.

Big Dixon called a halt after an hour's strenuous walking, during which he calculated we had covered three miles. After ten minutes we toiled on again, sweating heartily, and suffering continuously from the myriads of insects that buzzed about our ears, and bit us on every exposed part of our bodies.

It was during our third rest that the first incident occurred that was to presage disaster. All through our journey, our guide's conduct had been admirable. He had led us unhesitatingly upon our course, had willingly lent a hand in clearing our path and blazing the trail along which we had travelled, and though, as I have said, we sometimes heard movements of the concealed Spaniards near our route, he had made no attempt whatever to communicate with them. All this had helped to remove Big Dixon's suspicions. But somehow or other the Don loosed the rope that bound his waist. Of a sudden he sprang up, and made a dive to the edge of the clearing in which we sat. Like a flash, Dixon had levelled his pistol and aimed at the fleeing man. However, he did not fire, rushing off in chase of the man instead.

So quickly did all this happen that the rest of us had not even scrambled to our feet by the time Big Dixon had disappeared from view. To have followed would have been to court disaster. Our best plan, obviously, was to await Dixon's return, rather than lose touch with one another by pursuing a man already beyond our sight. This, therefore, we did, and to us, half an hour later, returned Big Dixon, sweating freely, but dispirited after a futile chase.

"What a fool I was," he cried, flinging himself down to the ground. "Even a landlubber could have tied a knot that he couldn't loose."

"Cheer up, Dick," said I. "What's done is done, and can't be altered. But why didn't you fire when you had him covered?"

"Because I didn't want to warn any Spaniards who might be in the neighbourhood. I thought I could have caught him, but he dodged under cover before I could overtake him. Pity I didn't wing him, as it's turned out."

We sat in gloomy silence for a while. It was Fiddler Jim who broke it.

"And what are we to do now, eh?"

It was indeed a problem. Prudence suggested that we should make our way back to Gibraltar. Yet to me the thought of turning back was impossible. I felt convinced that our guide had not brought us on entirely a wild-goose chase. Somewhere near us lay the English prisoners we sought, and, if Fate were kind, amongst them would be my father. How could I contemplate turning back at such a moment?

"What you men decide, I leave to you," said I. "For my own part, I'm going to scout around, and see if I can find any traces of our comrades."

Big Dixon scratched his head.

"'Tis rank foolishness, lad, but——"

His speech was cut short by the sudden crack of a musket, near at hand, and the whistle of a shot, as it passed close to our ears. We flung ourselves to earth, in case other muskets were covering us. There being no further report, Big Dixon gave the word, and we dashed for the cover of the woods. Once in their shelter, we wended our way in single file for perhaps half an hour, dodging this way and that, in an attempt to throw our enemies off our trail.

At last Big Dixon paused to rest, and we sat down, breathing heavily, for the pace had been severe. We did not dare to talk, even in whispers, until we felt certain that no enemies were near. Who knew what foes were hidden by the surrounding woods?

Instead, we lay, listening. I could hear the rapid, heavy thumping of my heart; the quick breathing of my companions, the rustle of the wind in the tree-tops, the cries of the birds; but of human foes, not a trace.

"I believe we've flung them off our track," whispered Big Dixon at length. "It now remains to decide what to do."

"What do you propose, Dick?" I asked.

"Well, Arthur, I'm ready to agree with you that we scout around before we consider returning to Gibraltar. I believe that Don was leading us aright, and delayed his own escape until he was near to a camp of his comrades, probably where the prisoners are kept."

"If that is so, Dick, as I believe, too, we may yet find that camp and release our friends."

"Ay, lad, unless the Spaniards capture us first."

This gloomy reflection kept us all silent for a little, but Big Dixon was too optimistic to be downcast for very long.

"Now this is what I propose," said he, "that we split up into two parties, three of us together, and the fourth to keep within earshot of the others. Three of us will scout round in search of the Spaniards' hiding-place—perhaps you noticed a beaten path we crossed in our run through the woods just now. It's more than likely that will lead us where we want to go."

"And the fourth man?" queried Fiddler Jim.

"'Twill be his job to spy unseen on the rest of us. If nothing happens to us, there's no harm done. But if the Dons fall upon us and capture us, it gives him a chance to bring a rescue party."

He turned to Fiddler Jim, and laid his hand upon his shoulder.

"Jim," said he seriously, "I'm going to ask you to be the fourth man. I promised Sir Hugh Ellis that I'd stick with Arthur here, and it's a promise I must keep. If the Dons attack and capture us, will you try to win back to Gibraltar, tell Captain Gentle—or Morgan, if he's back—and lead a party to our rescue?"

Fiddler Jim looked uncomfortable.

"I ain't much of a hero, I know," said he, "but I don't fancy the job you've given me. Looks too much like runnin' away."

"It's the worst job of the lot, Jim. You'll have to go back alone all the miles we've travelled, and be in danger every yard of the way."

"If you say it's the right thing for me to do, Dick, I'll do it." And the two men clasped each other's hands with a firm grasp.

Having seen our weapons were in good order, Big Dixon, Polly, and myself set off to look for the beaten path we had crossed in our mad haste through the woods. We each bade the disconsolate Jim farewell before we went, not knowing whether we should ever clap eyes upon him again.

We found the path without trouble, and tossed a piece of eight to decide which way we should traverse it to begin with. The toss told us to proceed westward, and we started in single file, Big Dixon, as usual, in the post of danger.

After perhaps half an hour's walking, we came to a bend in the path, which we rounded cautiously, to find a fallen tree-trunk lying across our way. This looked suspicious, but as there was no sign of foemen near we pressed on. Twenty yards from the tree, Big Dixon bade us halt while he went on alone to investigate. He had just reached the fallen tree, and had half turned to wave us onwards, when men broke from cover on either side and rushed towards us.

I caught a glimpse of Big Dixon returning at full speed, but after that all my energies were taken up in fighting. I found time to fire my pistol at the Spaniard who came full tilt at me, and experienced a wild thrill of joy when he dropped clean in his tracks. There was no opportunity to draw another weapon before a great, hair-covered fellow had seized me in a cruel grip.

Dimly to my ears came an ejaculation from Polly, "It's Pedro the Hairy!" That made me all the more anxious to escape. Desperately I kicked his shins, and dug my teeth savagely into the hand that was pressed against my mouth. The giant picked me up like a puppy, and after a vigorous shake, flung me to the ground, where I lay helpless, all the breath knocked out of me.

My comrades were still unsubdued. Polly was at grips with another of the Spaniards, while Big Dixon kept a number at bay by the vigorous wielding of his axe. Pedro the Hairy, having disposed of me so easily, turned his attention to Polly Flinder, whom he stunned with one terrific blow of his fist behind the ear.

Weak though I was, I managed to find my voice.

"Fly, Dick, fly. You can't help us by stopping."

Big Dixon half turned as though to attempt my rescue. Better counsel prevailed in the nick of time. He turned, knocked down one of the Dons who stood in his path, and next moment could be heard crashing his way through the undergrowth.

Pedro the Hairy gave rapid orders, and a number of the Dons started in pursuit. The rest turned to Polly and myself, and our arms were firmly tied behind us. While this was being done, I noticed our escaped guide was looking down at me with a malicious grin upon his face.

"So I was to suffer torture, boy, eh? Perhaps that will be your lot now."

I made no answer, but still he went on.

"Your big comrade will be caught, never fear. But there were four of you. Where is the little man, who sings, and bears a fiddle upon his shoulders?"

His reference to Fiddler Jim reminded me that the latter would have witnessed our capture, and doubtless already be on his way in search of a rescue party. It behoved me to give him the best chance of escape I could, so I replied that he had fallen down in our race for safety, and broken his leg. And I pretended to point out the direction in which we had left him in hiding—quite different, needless to say, from the direction he would actually have to take.

"We will find him," said the Spaniard, "and bring him to the place you wished to visit—to the place where we're going to take you—to where we keep the English slaves."

CHAPTER XI

PEDRO THE HAIRY

DIRECTLY Polly Flinders had recovered his senses, he and I were forced to our feet, and started on our journey to the prisoners' camp.

We entered it late in the afternoon. The path led us for several more miles through the forest, then emerged to cross a small, open plain. Beyond this the ground was rough and rocky. The camp stood at the top of a small hillock, where we found a natural platform some twenty yards square in extent. At various places on the slopes, rocks had been cunningly arranged. From below they appeared to be but a natural part of the scenery. Yet each was a little fort of its own, behind which three or four men could shelter, and fire upon an attacking force as the assailants clambered up the slope.

"I hope Pedro the Hairy don't recognise me," Polly managed to whisper, as we toiled up the last slope towards the camp.

The black-haired slave-driver had paid us but scant attention once we had been bound. He had reprimanded his followers for allowing Big Dixon to escape, but after that had said nothing, and had tramped away in front of us, striding along at a rare speed, so that it was difficult for Polly and me, bound as we were, to keep up with him. I could not help admiring the grand physique of the man. He was larger than Big Dixon, but more gracefully built, despite his great size. I felt that in him my friend would find his master if ever the twain should meet in a hand-to-hand fight.

Arrived in the camp, we were led to a ring formed of boulders, and flung rudely through the gap left as a doorway. Within we saw some half-dozen men, naked, bruised, emaciated, lying in chains upon the ground.

One of them turned upwards his drawn, unshaven face, in which the two eyes burned like fierce lights. He gave a sudden start of recognition.

"Why, it's young Arthur Ellis, split me sides! An' Polly Flinders."

I had to look at him again before I recognised him, so weak and changed was he. "Why, it's Swampy, isn't it?" I asked.

"The same, sir. Late master-gunner of the *Rover*. Now a slave, which is about ten times as bad as bein' a dog."

"Tell me," said I, as soon as Polly and I had exchanged greetings with him and the other slaves. "My father! Where is he?"

Swampy sadly shook his head.

"For all I know, young sir, he may be dead, as some of our messmates are, what with the blows, the toil, and the starvation. They took him an' the rest right across the isthmus, to Panama. Pray God he survived the journey."

To learn that my father was not in Maracaybo Lagoon, after all my hopes of seeing him again, was almost too much for me. I nearly forgot the manhood to which I aspired, and wept, but checked the impulse in time. Yet I dared not speak for a long while for fear of shaming myself.

Before we slept that night, Swampy gave me an account of what had happened to the prisoners after Polly's escape.

"They didn't discover he had gone until it was time for us to move next day, but there was the very devil to pay. Your father in particular was questioned, but not a word would he say. They flogged him, but still not a word. I tell you, boy, your father is the finest man I've ever clapped eyes on. Not one of us here but would cheerfully die for him."

And then I learned in fuller detail how my father had kept up the spirits of his fellow-slaves, how he had preached hope to them instead of despair, how he had done his best to soothe their hurt bodies as well as their spirits.

"Many's the time, when one of us was bein' flogged, that your father would shout out some insult to the striker, and bring the lash upon himself instead. But though time and again they thrashed him till he bled, they could never break his spirit. An' d'you know how he would comfort himself an' us more than any other way?"

He paused for a reply, but I shook my head, being afraid to speak lest I should burst into tears.

"Why, he used often to say, 'My boy an' Big Dixon have escaped, I'm sure o' that. An' they'll not forget us.' An' I, for one, believed it, lad. Little did I think you'd be brought to us, like ourselves, a prisoner."

So dismal was Swampy's voice, that I endeavoured to comfort him by telling of Big Dixon's escape from capture, and of Fiddler Jim's instructions to bring help from the buccaneers.

Dawn came, and with it fresh realisation of the danger in which we stood. About an hour after sunrise we were all lined up outside the circle of stones which had formed our prison. As we had been bound all night, you may guess that Polly and I were in great pain, and feeling very miserable. But when I looked round at the others, and noted the half-healed scars they bore, I felt how happy was my condition compared with theirs, and prayed that I might not be called upon to endure the horrible sufferings that had been their lot.

Presently Pedro the Hairy came striding across to where we stood. He was naked to the waist, and as I looked at the thick matted hairs which covered his gigantic torso, I was irresistibly reminded of a black bear I had once seen performing tricks. Just as savage, too, was his heart.

He held out his hand close in front of my eyes, and with satisfaction I saw that I had bitten it deeply in the fight of the previous day.

"Do you see what you did?" he snarled, and with a flick of his great paw sent me sprawling. Polly Flinders growled in his rage, and strained at his bonds, but only succeeded in attracting the brute's attention to himself.

Pedro turned to him, and gave a start as he peered at the bronzed face. He took hold of Polly's chin, and lifted his face upwards for a closer inspection.

"I've seen you before, you dog, I know," he roared.

With a sudden jerk he turned Polly round, and rent the shirt from his body. Across the whiteness of his back, plain to behold, were the scars of past lashes.

"Ah, ha!" roared the giant. "Here are signs of my own handiwork, I'll wager. No one but Pedro the Hairy crosses his marks like that. You—— I know you now. You're the slave who escaped."

Poor Polly! He tried to maintain a resolute

bearing, but I could guess at the sick fear that was clutching his heart.

"Well," said Pedro, after a minute's pause, "you have nothing to say. But I have—and I'll say it with a whip. Hola, Samba, bring me my lash."

A smiling negro brought forth the whip, and I shuddered as I saw it. Short of handle, but with long, tough, knotted thong, no wonder Polly blanched beneath his tan.

Pedro drew the long lash through his fingers, and grinned maliciously. Then round he swung it; the thong curled around his head, hissed out, and descended with tremendous force diagonally across Polly's back.

The seaman bit his lips, and choked back a groan, but there was a look of wild agony in his eyes. Again came the lash, hissing like some devilish live thing, and a second weal rose livid upon the flesh. The second weal made with the first the letter X.

"Pedro's mark!" yelled the Dons in delight, and the hairy brute preened himself in the warmth of their applause.

"Ay, Pedro's mark!" he cried, "and 'twill be repeated many times before I've done. I'll teach a slave under my command not to run away. Tie him up to the pole."

They loosed Polly's arms, and led him to an eight-foot pole that stood in one corner of the platform. Then his hands were again tied, this time high above his head. Pedro the Hairy prepared to continue the flogging.

There came the report of a musket, and the man standing next to Pedro fell forward with a low cry. At the same instant came a great figure bounding into view. It was Big Dixon, mad with anger. Before any could do aught to stay him he had covered the distance between Pedro and himself, and levelled the brute to earth with a full-blooded swing of his left fist.

Immediately a score of weapons were raised to strike down this bold intruder. Big Dixon snatched up a cudgel which lay on the ground nearby, determined to sell his life dearly. He would have stood no chance. It was the very man he had struck down who saved him.

"Don't harm him, but don't let him get away," commanded Pedro the Hairy from the ground.

He rose slowly, ruefully rubbing the place where Big Dixon's fist had struck him. Then he picked up his great whip, clutching the handle grimly.

"Never yet has there been man I've feared to meet," he growled. "Take his cudgel from him. Let him loose, but form a ring around so that he cannot escape. If he attempts to break the ring, shoot him—and shoot to kill!"

His instructions were obeyed. A clear space was formed in which Big Dixon and his antagonist could manœuvre. But whereas Dick was without weapons, Pedro the Hairy was armed with his formidable whip.

Swish! The long lash hissed outward, and bit into Dixon's shoulder. He attempted to dart in upon the slave-driver. Crack! It caught him across the chest, checking his rush straightway.

I came near to weeping during the next few minutes. Brave though Dixon was, desperately though he strove to reach his persecutor, he stood no chance. Again and again the lash seared his flesh. He could not penetrate beyond its cruel barrier. His clothes were ripped by its wild slashes and dyed with the blood from his hurts. I could see he was doomed to defeat.

All the same I was surprised when he dropped to earth so soon, shielding his face with his arms, but exposing his undefended back to the lash. I had thought his great strength would have enabled him to struggle longer. Leering with triumph, Pedro stepped forward, prepared to thrash his defeated antagonist into senselessness.

His over-confidence was his undoing. Like a rubber ball for quickness, Big Dixon jumped to his feet. Back staggered Pedro, anxious to put the whip's length between himself and his foe. Too late! Like a leopard springing at its prey, Big Dixon soared into the air in a stupendous leap. The lash met him in mid-air, but there was no staying him now. Full upon the hairy chest he landed, and back fell Pedro to the ground, his enemy upon him. Despite their danger, and the knowledge that the lash would presently sting them into silence, the prisoners raised a cheer at their persecutor's discomfiture.

But though Big Dixon had accomplished much in getting to grips with his opponent, he found himself locked in arms stronger than he had ever before met. Fortunately for Dick, the sudden fall had somewhat dazed the Don, giving my comrade the opportunity of securing a wrestler's hold. Yet when Pedro recovered, as he quickly did, he set himself to break the hold, tugging at Dixon's wrists with all his mighty strength.

Break the hold he did, at last, but by the time he had done so, he was gasping for breath. With a desperate heave he flung Big Dixon from him, and struggled to his feet. With joy in my heart I noticed that while Pedro's chest was heaving mightily, my comrade was comparatively fresh. He gave the Spaniard scant time for recovery.

He darted in at him, seized him low down, and, using his shoulder as a lever, tipped the Don over his head.

Pedro rose, and a grim, formidable figure he looked. His last fall had gashed his forehead badly, and a trickle of dark blood had run down his face and on to his hairy chest, adding to the menace of his appearance. With an impatient gesture, he dashed the blood from his eyes, at the same time shouting to his comrades, who were edging forward to aid him, to keep back.

He curled his huge hands, until they looked like the talons of some wild beast. I shuddered at the sight of his long, filthy nails.

With a quick spring he was upon Dixon, before the latter could leap to avoid him. Once, twice, his hands scored Dixon's flesh, leaving ugly scars behind. Then, opening wide his arms, and sweeping them round with tremendous power, he had caught Big Dixon in his great grasp, and was squeezing him against his chest. In a moment the Spanish onlookers' downcast looks had been replaced by smiles of jubilation. Big Dixon's arms were pinned against his sides, so that he could not move them, and he was slowly but surely being crushed to death in the bear-like grasp of the gigantic Pedro.

I thought all was over, but Big Dixon had fought many fights in his time, and knew every trick in the game. Being in desperate straits, he took a desperate chance to escape. After a few seconds, in which his quiescent body looked as though he had given up the struggle, he suddenly tautened his muscles, and fell stiffly backwards. Pedro had no time to prevent him, and had, perforce, to fall with him. And in falling, he did what Dixon had hoped and expected, that is, momentarily slackened his grasp. With a mighty effort Big Dixon burst the hold that had ensnared him; his knee bent upwards, and fixed itself on Pedro's stomach; a sudden heave of my comrade, and the Don went flying over his head. He fell heavily upon his shoulder. There came a snap like the crack of a whip, and Pedro lay still.

The moment's intense silence made the succeeding minutes of pandemonium deafening by contrast. Angered beyond measure at their champion's downfall, the other Spaniards rushed forward and seized Dixon before he could stagger to his feet. A noose was wrapped about his neck, and the other end of the rope flung over the cross-piece of a gallows already erected in the place.

A dozen willing hands seized the rope. The noose tightened upon Big Dixon's neck.

"Stop!" cried I, at the top of my voice, and there was such urgency in my tones that I was obeyed. "Listen!" One and all, as though struck motionless by a magician's wand, listened intently to the sound that had reached me, and inspired me to interfere.

Yes! I was not mistaken. Faintly borne upon the wind came the strains that often Fiddler Jim had played upon the *Rover's* deck, and many a time since:

"They rove a noose in a hempen rope,
They dropped it over his head, oh!
They jerked him up in a hangdog dance
Till Bobtail Dick was dead, oh!"

"Come, lads, let's join in the chorus! Let it rip, so that Fiddler Jim will hear. All together now."

They joined in with a will. The slaves, out of whom most of the spirit had been crushed during their servitude, started uncertainly, but swelled into greater volume as the prospect of rescue grew upon them. Big Dixon tore the noose from his neck, and joined in with his mighty bass:

"So heave away, with a roundelay,
(This be the song to sing, oh!)
We're off to sea, and we leave the tree
Where Bobtail Dick doth swing, oh!"

How we roared as there came a mighty cheer to greet our chorus! In vain the Spaniards strove to keep us silent! Only death would have done that, and the Dons hesitated to kill us, fearing the buccaneers' vengeance. One or two began to find a vantage-place from which they could fire upon the approaching buccaneers, but the majority were more in favour of retreat than fighting. They were confirmed in this desire by one of their scouts rushing in with the news that a large number of the buccaneers were approaching.

"If you flee, and leave us unharmed, I'll promise there shall be no pursuit. Only you must leave Pedro the Hairy to our vengeance!" I shouted.

My words appeared to decide them. Carrying their weapons only, they broke away in disorder, leaving their prisoners behind, and Hairy Pete stretched out upon the ground.

Big Dixon's first task was to cut the bonds of Polly and myself. He could not release the others' chains until keys were found, or irons to strike them off. He moved as though to signal to Fiddler Jim and his comrades, but turned back, and looked down doubtfully at the man he had beaten.

"If we leave him here, the buccaneers will torture him," he muttered.

"Doesn't he deserve torture?" asked Swampy bitterly. "Hasn't he made our lives miserable ever since we came under his hand?"

"Yet, for English seamen, there's little pleasure to be gained by hurting a helpless man. What say you, lads? This boy, Arthur, and I have run some risks in searching after you. Will you let us hide this fellow from the buccaneers?"

The other Englishmen made no immediate response. Dixon was asking a big thing of them to forego revenge on this bully who had ill-treated them for so many months. I felt wonderfully proud of them when Swampy, speaking for the rest, said:

"If you'd suffered what we have, Big Dixon, I don't think you'd ask. But as you have, I, for one, will agree. And the rest of you are with me, ain't you, lads?"

There came a growl of approval, not very enthusiastic, perhaps, but that was hardly to be expected. At any rate, it was enough for Big Dixon, who picked up his late opponent in his arms (a feat which taxed his own strength to the utmost) and staggered away with him to find some niche where his body might remain concealed. Hardly had he returned before the buccaneers, led by Captain Gentle and Fiddler Jim, came scrambling up the hillside, and rushed into the camp.

Fiddler Jim flung himself impulsively upon us, glad to find us alive, then turned to greet his old mess-mates of the *Rover*, whom he had hardly dared hope to see again. As for Captain Gentle, he stood scratching his head perplexedly.

"How's this, bullies?" he asked. "I thought you were in deadly danger?"

"So we were, sir, and it's thanks to your arrival we escaped. Our captors have run away, not ten minutes ago."

"Ay, cap'n," put in Swampy, "and if you search in yon cavern you'll find your visit here well worth while!"

It was, indeed, for investigation brought to light seven large caskets, each filled to the brim with precious stones and ornaments. So excited were the buccaneers at this discovery that they gave no thought to following the Spaniards, so that I had no difficulty in keeping the promise I had made to prevent pursuit.

"Knocker will look a pretty fool when he makes his complaint to Morgan," said Captain Gentle. "Not only have I the defence that I was keeping the Admiral's promise to you, Arthur, but these caskets of treasure would be excuse enough for a far worse crime."

The fetters having been struck from the limbs of the late slaves, and their hurts tended to, we began our return journey to Gibraltar, it being deemed unsafe to remain longer for fear the Spaniards might return in force. On the way back Fiddler Jim told us that no sooner had he seen us taken prisoners than he had started back for aid, as arranged. Twice he had lost his way, but had struggled into Gibraltar soon after midnight. While he snatched an hour's rest, Captain Gentle had rounded up his own men, and with very little delay the relief party had started off.

"I found my way as far as the tree where you were attacked," concluded Jim, "but after that it was largely a matter of guesswork. We followed the path, but in time it disappeared, and we hardly knew what to do. In despair I took out my fiddle hoping to let you know help was at hand if you were within hearing."

"'Twas a good job for me you played the old tune," said Big Dixon in a serious voice, "otherwise I should be by now the Bobtail Dick of the song," and he explained how near he had been to hanging.

We reached Gibraltar again before nightfall, to find Morgan returned and in a fearful temper; not with us, fortunately, but with Knocker for refusing us aid. Besides this, he had learned through his spies that the fort at the entrance of the lagoon was almost completely reconditioned, and our chance of escape comparatively small.

In spite of this, the buccaneers lingered in and around Gibraltar for five weeks in all. During this time, frightful tortures continued to loosen the tongues of the Spaniards taken prisoner, and fresh hoards of wealth were brought to light, until sufficient booty had been collected to ensure the expedition being hugely successful if only the spoils could be taken back to Port Royal.

Therein lay the trouble. When eventually we arrived back at Maracaybo, an envoy awaited us from the Spanish commander who had rebuilt and re-equipped the fort, Don Alonso del Campo y Espinosa. The envoy coolly informed us that three Spanish warships lay inside the entrance to the lagoon to prevent our departure. If by any stroke of good fortune we succeeded in evading those, we still had the guns of the fort with which to contend. But the Spanish commander wished to be generous. If we restored all the booty and prisoners we had taken, and gave up our arms, we would be allowed to return unharmed to Jamaica.

Admiral Morgan parleyed for a little, but I knew all the time that, desperate though our position was, he had no intention of agreeing to the offered terms. He sent the envoy back with an indefinite answer, so as to gain time to confer with his captains.

"You've led me into a pretty trap in our search for your father," he said to me jestingly that night when I brought him in his evening meal. "Don't you think it's up to you to find a way out of the trap?"

"If I suggest a plan, will you promise to lead an expedition to Panama?" I asked eagerly.

Morgan looked at my excited face, and smiled reassuringly.

"I shall escape from this trap, never fear," said he, "and this, moreover, I swear. If death does not take me (as I feel it will not for many a long year) I will do what Francis Drake tried to do, but failed. I will lead my men across the isthmus to Panama. There is something within me that urges me onward. It is my destiny. Who can escape what has been planned for him?"

Satisfied that Morgan would attempt the march to Panama, I decided to talk the matter over with Big Dixon. I found him, with Fiddler Jim and the other survivors from the *Rover*, huddled round a smoky fire, endeavouring to protect themselves against the swarms of mosquitoes which were a continual plague on the islands and coast of the Spanish Main.

Briefly I outlined a plan, which was based upon the method by which Sir Francis Drake had first disorganised the great Spanish Armada in the days of Queen Bess. As I spoke I recalled the thrills that used to assail me when Dominie Brabacombe told us that thrilling story—how the English fire-ships, laden with combustibles, were sailed in amongst the great galleons, and left there, ablaze, to shatter the Spanish dream of conquering England—till we scholars became almost delirious with pride, and vowed with mighty oaths that we, too, would go to sea and lower the Spanish power. Little had I thought, then, as I sat upon the hard school bench, that it would be my lot to join with desperate buccaneers against the hated foe.

"Let us fill our oldest ship," said I, "with fire-balls, oil, and combustibles of all kinds. Send her straight for the largest Spanish galleon. Ten to one the Spaniard will grapple with her, which will mean her doom."

Big Dixon shook his head dubiously.

"What about a crew? Even the buccaneers will not volunteer to sail upon a fire-ship which will mean them being roasted to death. And if no men are visible upon deck, the Dons will be suspicious, and keep away."

"I've thought of that, Dick. We can make a dummy crew—logs of wood will do the trick. Dress 'em up in the buccaneers togs, arm them with our oldest cutlasses and burst muskets. The Dons will imagine the ship is crowded with buccaneers ready to board 'em, and they'll have no thought of fire-ships. Mark my words—what's that?"

My ear had caught the sound of stealthy movements just outside our bivouac. Big Dixon and I simultaneously sprang for the entrance, and collided with each other. The slight delay was long enough for the listener, whoever he was, to get clear away. I caught a glimpse of some one moving, far away in the shadows, but it would have been hopeless to follow.

"An eavesdropper, eh?" said Big Dixon. "Now I wonder whom it could have been?"

CHAPTER XII

TRAPPED IN MARACAYBO LAGOON

NEXT morning, early, I was summoned to the council, where the captains sat to decide how best to win clear of the trap in which they found themselves.

Of course my presence was required there to supply the wants of the buccaneers and not to join in their deliberations. For all that I determined, if given the chance, to propose the plan I had already suggested to Big Dixon.

Knocker sat down just as I entered, amid general applause. When this had somewhat subsided, I heard my own name shouted, and bore my flagon of wine towards Morgan's seat.

"Here's a lad who told me he has a plan to extricate us from our difficulties!" roared Morgan, his eyes a-twinkle. "Up you get on yonder cask, my lad, and tell us your scheme. It may be better than that of Knocker!"

Nothing loth (for all my nervousness) I stepped on to the upturned brandy cask, and gazed at the faces around through shrouds of tobacco smoke. Captain Gentle's face wore a reassuring grin, while Knocker greeted my glance with a scowl, yet for all that there was a hint of amusement in his eyes.

"My plan is a simple one," I began. "Load your poorest ship with combustibles. Dress up logs of wood to represent the crew. Sail her——"

My words were drowned by such a howl of derision that I hastily jumped down from my rostrum, wondering in what way I had blundered. Presently I was aware of Knocker upon his feet.

"Didn't I say this youngster was listening outside my tent last night when I talked over the plan with Diaz here? But little did I think he would have the calm impudence to put forward my plan as the effort of his own puny brain. It's high time the lad was taught his place. You too often give him kind words, Admiral, instead of a rope's-end."

"Ay!" growled Diaz, a villainous-looking fellow who was reputed to know the path across the isthmus to Panama. "The lad was skulking outside like a thief last night. Let him be flogged, Admiral, and taught that a boy's place is not to push himself in amongst his betters."

Dumbfounded I listened to the angry words directed against me. I realised all too clearly now who had been the eavesdropper of the previous evening. Naturally the buccaneers thought it more likely that an experienced fighter like Knocker should think of such a plan than that a raw boy like myself should do so; hence their anger and the evil looks they cast me. Even Morgan was scowling, and of all the buccaneers present only Captain Gentle still looked at me with friendly eyes.

"Why all this fuss?" asked he, jumping to his feet. "What matter whose plan it is? Couldn't they both have thought of the same idea? Let's decide whether to carry it out, say I, for the sooner we win clear of Maracaybo Lagoon the healthier it will be for all of us."

His words had their effect, and I was able to withdraw without further suggestions of punishment. An hour later the council broke up. All the buccaneers were summoned, and the Admiral briefly explained to them how it was proposed to win clear of Maracaybo Lagoon. Then working parties were organised. Some of the men were given the task of clearing the oldest vessel of all the equipment worth saving. Others had to load it with combustibles, so arranging the deadly cargo that any sudden shock would set the ship on fire, when, so liberally was it bedaubed with oil, that it would speedily be ablaze from fore to aft. The job that caused the chief amusement was the preparation of the fire-ship's crew. Logs of wood were hewn, and clad in old clothes of the buccaneers. Sombreros were drawn over the coloured handkerchiefs which crowned each dummy, and "Knocker's buccaneers" (as they were nicknamed) were placed in suitable positions on deck or in the yards and riggings of the fire-ship. Some of the humorists of the buccaneers completed their task by decorating the dummies with tremendous whiskers and painting upon them noses, eyes, and scars.

All was in readiness by late afternoon. Prisoners and booty were packed in longboats, each in charge of a dozen buccaneers, heavily armed. The ships of the fleet, other than the fire-ship, were made ready for action, and Admiral Morgan issued instructions that no quarter was to be given or asked.

"And if any of your mates shows the white feather," he added, "strike him down. We're in desperate straits, my lads, and only desperate courage can take us to freedom."

The fleet set sail, the fire-ship in the van. Presently we came in sight of the grey fort which frowned upon the entrance to the lagoon, and there, in the entrance, lay the great Spanish ships-of-war, each of them sufficiently powerful, if manned by a courageous crew, to have challenged our whole fleet.

Before long a cannon boomed a message of warning from the fort, and Captain Gentle, looking through his glass, reported that boats were leaving shore for the men-o'-war. "They're recalling those of the crew that had landed," said he, "an' pretty soon they'll be standin' off to meet us." Sure enough, the Spanish galleons presently left their moorings beneath the shelter of the fort, and began to bear in our direction.

"'Twill be a night action if the moon be fair," quoth Big Dixon, who stood with me in the bow of Gentle's ship, upon which Morgan had taken his quarters. "Night will fall before we're within gunshot." In the last part of his remark he was right. Before the gunners of either side had wasted powder and shot at extreme range, the sun sank behind the woods of the island, and darkness spread over land and sea with uncanny swiftness. But any hope of a night attack was quickly dispelled. So black was the night, unrelieved by moon and stars, that Morgan, reckless though he was, ordered the fleet to anchor rather than risk attempting to win free from the lagoon in the darkness. The Spaniards, it transpired, dared shift their position no more than we, for morning found both fleets in the same place that evening had left them.

Each ship of the buccaneer fleet was ready for action at break of day. The fire-ship was under way, and bearing down upon the Spanish galleons followed by a favouring breeze, before a movement could be discerned upon their decks. But long before the fire-ship had come up with them, their sails were trimmed, and they continued their advance.

The leading Spanish galleon, a vessel carrying forty guns, opened the battle with a shot which fell alongside our fire-ship, sending a fountain of spray splashing against its side.

"Let's hope their gunners don't score a hit," said Morgan, who was standing at my side, watching eagerly the Spaniards' tactics. "We don't want Knocker's fire-ship to fly sky-high before its time."

"Reckon the Dons will be marvelling at the courage of 'Knocker's buccaneers,'" cried Gentle, with a chuckle. "Logs of wood will stand a cannonade better than flesh and blood, I'll swear."

To Morgan's relief, and the joy of the rest of the buccaneers, no further shot was aimed at our fire-ship, which by now had far outstripped the rest of our fleet. Hopes ran high when it was seen that the leading galleon was approaching the fire-ship, evidently meaning to lay it aboard; and when grappling irons were flung, and the two vessels actually bumped together, the buccaneers let loose such a concerted yell of triumph as must have reached the very garrison of the fort.

This yell would have warned the galleon that some treachery was afoot, even if they had not discovered it through the wind dislodging some of the sombreros from "Knocker's buccaneers." But the warning was all too late. The bumping of the fire-ship against the galleon's side had been quite enough to set the inferno ablaze. Before the grappling irons could be released, flames were mounting from the decks of the fire-ship and leaping aboard the Spanish galleon. Ever and anon explosions were heard, wreaking destruction upon both vessels. Never before in my life had I seen a ship so quickly doomed as was the Spanish galleon.

The Dons themselves quickly realised the futility of attempting to save their vessel, and instead tried to save their lives. Two or three boats were lowered, but for the most part the Dons essayed to escape by swimming to the shore. Vain hope! Morgan's ships sailed in amongst the bobbing heads, and the buccaneers lined the bulwarks, making bets as they fired at the swimmers. In less than a quarter of an hour the whole of that galleon's crew had been wiped out of existence!

Menwhile, alarmed at the sudden disaster which had overtaken its leader, the second galleon was headed straight for the shore, and there beached. Morgan ordered a half-dozen boats in pursuit, but before these could reach land, the Spaniards had themselves set fire to their vessel and made their escape inland.

As for the third galleon, that had turned tail and run back to the fort. Without waiting for orders, Knocker set off in chase, and Morgan ordered our own vessel to do likewise. But presently heavy gun-fire from the fort warned us that it would be risking our ships to follow farther, so both our vessels abandoned the chase while yet beyond range of the Spaniards' shore-guns.

"All the same," said Morgan, "why should we let even one escape out of three? Into the boats, my hearties, and we'll make a clean sweep of things."

Big Dixon, myself, and the other survivors of the *Rover* found ourselves in Gentle's boat, pulling lustily for the galleon, which, now that it was under the protection of the land guns, turned at bay. On either side of us, other boats were urged along by lusty arms, the spirits of the buccaneers being at highest pitch. Though shot from ship and shore fell thickly about us, no heed was taken by the reckless attackers. Even when one shot fell plump aboard the boat that was racing us neck and neck, sinking it in a moment, the occupants of the other boats only roared out a howl of fury, and pulled the harder at their oars.

As we came nearer the galleon, the fire from the fort slackened, lest an inaccurate shot might fall aboard the Spanish vessel. For all that our danger was not lessened. Instead of the heavy shot came the whistle of musket-balls as the Spanish seamen fired steadily in our direction, being themselves sheltered by their bulwarks. To add to our task, boats could be seen putting off from the shore, bearing reinforcements.

I think that had we attacked in calmer mood, we should have failed. The very fact that we did not realise the odds we were facing gave us strength and courage to take us through the inferno of fire to the galleon's side, and we were scrambling upwards towards the deck before the first boatload of Spaniards had covered half the distance separating the ship from the shore.

A dark, scowling face confronted me as I scrambled upwards, and a blade came whizzing down towards me. Fortunately the man that struck could not reach me, for all that he leaned so far over the bulwarks that it was a marvel he did not overbalance. Seeing my advantage, I clutched hold of a projecting portion of the vessels' side with my left hand, while I aimed my pistol with the right. A moment later the Spaniard plunged seaward, nearly making me lose my hold as his body grazed mine in its fall.

In spite of the delay, I was one of the first to reach the deck, to find the Dons putting up a determined resistance. Captain Gentle, Big Dixon, some half-dozen others, and Morgan himself were aboard before me, and with pistols primed and cutlasses drawn, resolutely faced the Spaniards until their comrades should be ready to support them. But seeing a score or so of the Spaniards drop to knee, with levelled muskets, Morgan realised that to wait might mean death to all the buccaneers already on deck. Wherefore, with a wild cry of, "Forward, my hearties! Don't wait to be shot!" he darted onward with whirling blade, closely followed by his daring companions.

This unexpected charge quite disturbed the marksmen's aim, and those bullets that were fired mostly flew wide. Morgan had bowled over two of the Dons before any moved to oppose him, but the surprise once over, our little party was quickly hemmed in, and the cutlass blades played a merry tune about us. I found myself wedged in between Captain Gentle and the Admiral, both of whom were such doughty fighters that for many minutes I had no chance to show my courage or my boyish skill. Presently, however, Morgan, in leaning forward to return the thrust of a Spaniard who had pressed him hard, slipped on the blood bedaubed deck, and pitched upon his face. With the reckless courage of youth I bestrode him, opposing my weak blade to the swords of three Spanish officers, who had apparently picked out Morgan for our leader. My fate must have been death had not Big Dixon snatched me back out of harm's way, and himself pressed so vigorously upon the Dons that Morgan was given the chance to rise. Before Big Dixon could be stabbed from behind as a reward for his temerity, there came a hearty yell from the remaining buccaneers, who had been assembling upon deck, and they swept forward with such irresistible determination that all resistance fell before them. Such of the Spaniards as had escaped being cut down flung away their weapons, and made a dash for the side to fling themselves desperately into the sea.

The buccaneers would have seized muskets and fired upon the escaping Dons, but Morgan knew there was no time to be lost.

"Quit that, my hearties," he bawled. "Hauling on ropes, not fighting, is the job at present. We'll take this galleon from under the very guns of the fort to make up for the fire-ship we made a present of to the Dons."

And so we did! No doubt the commander of the fort did not at once realise the galleon had fallen into our hands. At anyrate, her bow had been turned away from shore, and she was well on her way to join the buccaneer ships, before the Spaniards opened fire upon us. Three shots only fell aboard us, doing but little damage, and amid cries of triumph from the buccaneers who had not joined in the boat attack, the galleon was brought out in safety to augment Morgan's fleet.

No sooner had the Spanish vessels been so thoroughly dealt with than Morgan signalled for his officers to join him upon Gentle's ship.

"Well," cried Knocker, holding on high his

goblet of wine, "here's success to the Brotherhood! We've soon swept away these galleons that sought to bar our passage."

Morgan rested his hand upon the speaker's wrist before he could drink.

"True enough, Knocker. But remember we're not out of danger yet. The fort still bars our passage to the open sea!"

Villain though Knocker was, I could not but admire his flashing eyes and reckless bearing as he removed Morgan's hand, and drank to his toast. "It's true enough the fort bars our way," said he, "but surely if we've brains enough to outwit the Spaniards once, we can again." And contemptuously he flung his goblet to the floor.

A hearty growl greeted his words. Knocker was always one who liked to bask in the sun of popularity, and this reception to his words made him continue.

"Didn't this young sea-lawyer suggest the same plan that I did for destroying the galleons?" he cried, pushing me with his foot as I stooped to pick up his goblet, so that I sprawled foolishly upon the floor. "What says his lordship? Has he any plan to allow us to sail in safety in spite of the fort?"

Red-faced I rose to my feet.

"Yes," said I defiantly, "I have a plan. And this time you can't very well forestall me, for I did not mention it two nights ago when you heard me speak of the fire-ship."

A yell of delight greeted my bold words. "There's a challenge for ye, Knocker," cried one, while another remarked, "Let's hear any plan you've got first, Knocker, then we'll find out if the boy has a better."

"Do you want me to be matched against a youngster like that?" asked he, with a scowl. "If I suggest a scheme, he'll likely enough say he thought of the same thing."

But Captain Gentle overruled this objection by bawling out, "Let the youngster be sent on deck till we've heard what Knocker has to propose. Then let the lad return, and we'll choose between the two plans."

This suited me well enough, though I judged from the scowl upon Knocker's face that it pleased him not at all. As it turned out, he had nothing to propose beyond a suggestion that the buccaneering ships should run the gauntlet of the fort's guns during the blackness of the night. Therefore the captains listened all the more intently to what I had to say when I was recalled to the cabin.

"Well, sir!" I began, addressing myself principally to the Admiral, "I hope that Captain Knocker and I haven't hit upon the same plan this time."

"It's likely enough," cried Gentle, with a deep laugh. "Nary a one of us but could have thought of the plan he's put forward."

"Let's hear yours, boy," said Morgan. "If it's worth following I shall be still further in your debt—but I'll not forget the repayment, never fear."

"Well, sir, if we can get the Dons to move their guns to the landward side of the fort——"

"If we could, we could slip out of this trap unscathed. But how to do it, boy, is the question."

"Let boats ply to the shore from our ships, sir. Let them go fully loaded, plain for the

Spanish watchers to see. Let them be pulled back by a couple of rowers apiece. The Spaniards will think we are landing a large party to attack them from the shore side. Actually the men we land can return after each trip lying hidden in the bottom of the boats."

There was a brief silence following my hastily sketched plan. Admiral Morgan himself led the buzz of approval that presently broke out by slapping his hand vigorously upon his thigh, and exclaiming that my plan was to save them all. Knocker alone tried to invent reasons for its failure, but his objections were swept aside, and commands given for the plan to be put into operation.

The buccaneers joined in the business with gusto. Boats loaded with armed men pulled time and again into the wooded creek ashore, and returned (or so a distant observer would have said) empty save for the rowers. Actually the same party was apparently landed again and again. On returning to our vessels, a boat would run alongside so that it was hidden from the fort by the ship it visited, whereupon the buccaneers hidden in the bottom would once again take their places on the thwarts.

For several hours this game was carried on. I think it was Captain Gentle who suggested that the Spaniards would be more than ever convinced that we intended to attack if an envoy were sent to them demanding a ransom, in return for which he would sail away and leave them unmolested. Because he knew Spanish well, and was bold enough for all his villainy, Knocker was chosen for the task, and as his boat left the ship's side I was foolish enough to jump down into it.

"Hello, planner of fine schemes," he greeted me, scowling the while, "are you thinking of coming with me to interview the commander of yonder fort?"

I made no reply, having no desire to do anything of the kind, whereupon he took it upon himself to sneer at me, which was unmanly of him, seeing I was only a boy.

"Perhaps you're afraid he might hang us up as a warning to Morgan and the rest. Envoys have been treated so before. So as you're afraid, don't you——"

"Nay, I'm not afraid," interrupted I, "and will come with you if I may."

He said no more, but when presently the boat's keel grounded upon the sand he beckoned to me to follow. Now it had struck me that as he loved me so little, he might intend me harm when there were no witnesses near. Wherefore my hand closed about the butt of a pistol I had secreted within my shirt front, and I followed him a couple of paces in the rear.

He did not deign to converse with me as we went (which annoyed me not a whit) nor did he attempt to molest me (which relieved me mightily). At length we stood in front of the massive gateway of the fort, holding aloft a white flag, and demanding audience of Don Alonso de Campo y Espinosa.

In due course the gate was opened, we were hurriedly ushered within, and the gate promptly barred behind us. Evidently the Dons had no intention of being the victims of a surprise attack.

As we crossed the outer courtyard, both Knocker and I used our eyes, and to our delight saw that the Dons had been deceived as had been intended. Already many of their great guns had been mounted upon the landward side of the defences, and other pieces were being man-hauled from the seaward mountings.

We found Don Alonso the tall, haughty, courageous señor we might have expected from his name and reputation. When Knocker, in an insolent speech, demanded a huge ransom in return for Morgan's promise not to take the fort, the Spaniard's dark eyes flashed angrily.

"Don't think," said he, "that this fort is now manned by the same sort of men that ran away when first your vessels forced an entrance into the Maracaybo Lagoon. They were poltroons, out and out, and I thank you for the tortures you have inflicted upon such as fell into your power. But though your ships easily won a way into yonder lagoon, they will find it a different matter to fight their way out."

"Yet where are your three men-o'-war that tried to bar our path?" asked the buccaneer banteringly. "Two burnt to blackened skeletons, and the other manned by our lads. To save your fortress being razed to the ground—as it will be to-night if you refuse—a hundred thousand doubloons is no heavy price."

"If you can capture this fort," was the grim response, "you are welcome to destroy it. As to ransom, not a single coin will you get from me. Yet my former offer still holds good. Restore your prisoners, and the spoil you have taken, and your ships may depart, this time, unharmed."

"Your offer is too generous, Señor Commander. When I return again, it will be cutlass in hand."

"And then, Señor Buccaneer, I shall be ready to meet you in fitting fashion. But tell your Admiral not to send you as envoy again. If he does, I swear by the Holy Saints to hang you high above our battlements as a warning to your comrades."

This haughty threat closed the interview, and we departed from the fort leaving the men of the garrison still striving lustily at their task of moving their guns from the positions that commanded the passage to the open sea.

CHAPTER XIII

THE WITCH OF PORT ROYAL

At first on leaving the fort we walked in silence. Knocker strode along in front, and I, still fearing treachery, followed him with hand upon pistol butt. And as I walked, I traced once again in imagination all that had befallen me since that fateful day upon the *Rover* when Spanish galleons had been sighted ahead and astern.

My musings were rudely interrupted by Knocker suddenly turning in his tracks and rushing at me. Instinctively my pistol was drawn from my shirt front, but my aim was wild. I had allowed my thoughts to wander, and paid the penalty by being caught off my guard. Knocker gripped me by the throat with one hand, whilst his other seized my pistol wrist, and a quick twist made me drop the weapon and utter a cry of pain.

He crooked his leg behind my knees and flung me backwards. As I fell, I wrenched my hand free from his grasp, and snatched at the knife-hilt that projected from his waist-band. A quick thrust wounded him slightly in the arm, but he soon had me helpless upon my back, while he held my arms to the ground by kneeling upon them.

"Now, my young jackanapes, we can settle accounts," he growled.

He rudely untied the neckerchief I wore, and with it, despite my struggles, bound my hands firmly together. Then he hauled me roughly to my feet, and grinned into my face.

"So you would suggest plans to Morgan, would you? You would venture to accuse me of eavesdropping, eh?"

As he spoke his eyes burned so fiercely that my strength left me, and I had much ado to keep from weeping. I felt that my last moments had come; and what was bitterest to me was the thought that I should be unable to bear the help to my father he was awaiting.

"I've little time to spare on your departure from this world," went on Knocker. "If you want to say a prayer, it must be brief. After that——"

Without finishing his sentence, he turned to pick up the knife that lay upon the ground. In a desperate effort to escape him I sprang up and fled, though my arms were bound tightly in front of me. It was, of course, hopeless to escape by flight, but when confronted by death a man will twist and turn in his efforts to escape, just as a rat in a wire-cage, plunged under water, will swim to and fro, to and fro, so long as life remains, vainly seeking a way out.

There came an angry cry from behind me, and the noise of running feet in pursuit. Panting with fear, I plunged into a clump of bushes that loomed up ahead.

A hand fell upon my shoulder, and drew me to one side. I recognised the huge bulk of Big Dixon. And then came Knocker, thundering behind. Big Dixon flung his crooked arm round the other's neck as he passed, and gave a sudden jerk which flung the buccaneer heavily to the ground.

With a snarl, Knocker was upon his feet, ready to cope with his new antagonist. Seeing the stature of his opponent, he drew pistol to fire, but Big Dixon swung his foot upwards in a vigorous kick, and sent the weapon flying. In rushed Knocker, thinking to catch my comrade unbalanced, but Dixon was wary, and greeted the charge by a quick hop to one side. As Knocker turned, a terriffic blow, straight from the shoulder, crashed home upon his chest.

Though I had but little doubt as to how the struggle would end, I judged it prudent to arm myself, and so stooped to pick up the fallen pistol. When I rose again, I found Dixon had darted forward and seized the other in his great arms. In vain might Knocker seek to break away; Dixon's huge muscles swelled up under the brown skin of his arms, and I knew that it needed a stronger man than the buccaneer captain to struggle out of that grasp.

Yet I was reckoning without a knowledge of the many tricks Knocker had at his disposal. I saw his head droop and his body sag, and thought his strength had left him. So, too, thought Big Dixon, and turned his head in my direction as though to ask what he should do to his foe. His averted head gave the buccaneer the chance he wanted. The limp form became suddenly full of energy; a desperate wrench nearly dragged him free of the encircling arms; at the same time he snapped at Dixon with open jaws, like a hound, and dug his teeth deep into my comrade's throat.

This so surprised Dixon that he unloosed his arms, and a second later Knocker was darting away for safety as fast as his legs would carry him. Bound though I was, I took a quick shot at his vanishing form, and had the satisfaction of seeing him leap into the air and continue thereafter limping with the left leg. Yet his flight was maintained at unchecked speed. Big Dixon made, at first, to follow his opponent, but realising he was no match for the other in fleetness of foot, turned back, the while he tenderly stroked his injured throat.

"I'll wring his neck for this," he growled angrily, as he loosened my bonds.

"Best not," I advised him. "You know Morgan won't tolerate fighting without his sanction and you mustn't forget that Knocker is one of the most useful men the Admiral has in his command."

I doubt if my words made any impression upon Big Dixon, who was in a mighty ill-temper, and growled about Knocker's foul trick during the remainder of our walk to the shore. Fortunately for the treacherous buccaneer, he had already made his report to Morgan, and had been rowed aboard his own ship. We found the vessels about to weigh anchor, ready to make the trip through the narrow passage to the open seas. For the time being my comrade was forced to nurse his wrath (as well as his injured neck) and mutter threats as to what he would do with Knocker when next he had him in his power.

Morgan called me down into his cabin, and I was at first tempted to tell him of the treacherous attack Knocker had made upon me, but when the Admiral began rating me for having been absent without his leave, I judged the time for complaints to be unpropitious. Acutally the Admiral was more concerned about my safety than angry at my desertion from duty. He reminded me that if I should suffer death or capture by the Spaniards, the chance of my father being released would vanish. "As you know, boy," said he, "I'm a very superstitious man. It was once told me by the witch of Port Royal—an old, bent dame is she, who sits in the rum-shop I frequent—that it would be my fate to march to Panama. And I've never forgotten her last words, 'You'll be led by a villain; you'll walk beside the son of an old friend; you'll be deceived by the man you trust most. All these things must be for you to succeed!'"

"A strange prophecy, sir," said I. "How does the rest of it fit in?"

"The first part, well enough. Diaz, the fellow who led us to Gibraltar, reckons he knows the path to Panama, and promises to lead my men if I make it worth his while. He's villain enough, I'll wager, but likely to be useful for all that. It's the last part of her prophecy that I cannot believe. If you asked me which of my officers I trust above all others, I'd answer Captain Bradley. You haven't met him yet, boy, I believe, but I'd stake my life upon his loyalty."

"Are you sure he's the one you trust most?" I asked.

"Certain! After him—but a long way after—comes Captains Gentle and Knocker. But Captain Bradley I trust most, and I swear, witch or no witch, he'll never abuse my trust."

As soon as night fell, sails were set, and at a given signal our vessels steered for the passage. There was silence upon every deck. Had all the guns been moved from the seaward defences of the fort? Should we gain the open sea without a single shot to dispute our passage? As the vessels moved silently forward, one and all waited eagerly for an answer to these questions.

As befell the commander of the enterprise, the Admiral's vessel assumed the post of chief danger, last of the line. The first vessel, dimly seen far ahead, sailed within gunshot of the fort. The second followed, then the third. No angry boom of a gun awoke the night air. Silently, like ghosts, one by one our vessels made the passage. At last came our turn. Slowly we drew abreast of the silent fort, the commander of which had boasted we should never sail out of the lagoon of Maracaybo.

I could imagine his chagrin as he watched us slipping out of his grasp. I could see in imagination his men straining like fiends at the guns in a frenzied attempt to move them once again to their platforms overlooking the lagoon entrance. Whatever their efforts, the Spaniards were too late. Quite unmolested, the Admiral's ship, last of the fleet, passed the fort. As a last act of mingled defiance and boasting, Morgan gave orders for a broadside to be emptied into the silent fort ere we sailed away.

It was a proud fleet that sailed into Port Royal two days later, and a roaring trade the rum-shops did when the buccaneers got ashore. Tongues wagged as freely as the liquor flowed, and many was the mock toast drunk to the Spanish commander who had been so easily fooled.

Directly the ships cast anchor I went ashore, as in duty bound, to pay a visit to Sir Thomas Modyford. I found that the Governor was indisposed and abed. As the doctor's orders were that he was not to be disturbed, I sought out my old tutor, who welcomed me with tears in his eyes.

"I've missed you so much, Arthur," he said, and there was no mistaking his sincerity. "I've thought of you amongst all those rough men"—here poor Algy shivered as he remembered his own unpleasant experiences during the expedition to Porto Bello—"and I've been blaming myself for not having gone with you."

"Indeed," said I, "but I thought you——"

"You thought I was afraid of mixing with the buccaneers? So I was and am. But for the love of you, boy, I'd do harder things than sail again with Morgan."

I pressed his hand in silence. I could not find words to express my admiration of this man, so ill-suited to hardships and fighting, who was yet willing to undergo them voluntarily for my sake.

"But what news, Arthur? Your father—is he——?"

"Still alive, sir, so far as I know, but at present beyond my power to aid." And I told Algy all I had learned of my father's fate.

Algy looked grave when I told him that Morgan purposed to attempt the passage to Panama, and that I would go with him. "I'm afraid, lad, that Sir Thomas Modyford will not have the power, even if he has the will, to permit such an enterprise."

"But why? He said himself that he would——"

"Haven't you heard? It is freely rumoured here that peace has been patched up between Spain and England. If that is true, the commissions granted to Morgan and other buccaneers, allowing them to prey upon Spanish ships and towns, will be withdrawn."

"But would that prevent them carrying on?" I asked.

"To do so would make them no better than pirates, the enemies of all nations, Spain, France, and England alike. Any buccaneer then caught would be hanged at his own yard-arm as an outlaw. At present a buccaneer captain is treated as an officer in the English Navy, not as a pirate."

My heart fell within me. So this was to be the end of my proud determination to carry help to my father.

A sudden thought sprang into being.

"Suppose he sets sail again before he sees Sir Thomas. Suppose he never learns, at least officially, that Spain and England are at peace. Then he cannot be accused of piracy on his return, can he?"

Algy seized me by the shoulders in delight.

"You've hit on the only way, boy. We must see Morgan at once, and get him to start right away."

"We?" I asked. "Do you mean——?"

"I mean that I'm coming with you. There's no time like the present. Let's set off in search of the Admiral at once."

We picked up Big Dixon, Polly Flinders, and several others of the *Rover's* crew who had escorted me to the Governor's house, and had been sampling his wine in the servants' quarters. We knew the Admiral's favourite rum-shop, and made at once for the quayside where it was situated. As we passed along the street we saw, on either side, evidences of what was happening to the loot that had been brought from Gibraltar and Maracaybo. Every rum-shop was full to overflowing with the newly-returned buccaneers, and the acquaintances they had picked up ashore who were ready both to listen to their tales and help them to spend their money. Quarrels were frequent, and we passed more than one body of a buccaneer slain in a drunken quarrel. Other buccaneers lay about sleeping off the effects of drink. Still others danced and sang in drunken revelry. It was certain that whatever Morgan might wish to do, few of his men would be fit to sail with him until a dozen hours had passed to give them a chance to recover somewhat from their wild debauchery.

As we approached the Admiral's rum-shop, the strains of a fiddle could be heard scraping out the well-known tune:

> "They rove a noose in a hempen rope,
> They dropped it over his head, oh!
> They jerked him up in a hangdog dance
> Till Bobtail Dick was dead, oh!"

and it was followed by the chorus, twice repeated, sung with such full-throated enthusiasm, and accompanied by such a tremendous thumping of pots upon table-tops, and stamping of feet upon the wooden floor, that the very houses around seemed to shake with the clamour.

We made our way into the rum-shop, and as I was known to most of the men present, it was an easy task to force my way to where Fiddler Jim occupied a post of honour atop one of the tables, on which a chair, draped with a red cloth, had been placed.

As he saw the urgency of my manner, he quit fiddling and leaned over towards me.

"What is it, boy?" he asked. "News of your father?"

"No, Fiddler, but it's on his business. Do you know where I can find the Admiral?"

Fiddler jerked his thumb over his right shoulder.

"Sleepin' in his room yonder, though how he manages it with all this noise beats me. These fellows have no ear for a tune. They must be drowning my music with their stamping and yelling."

Leaving Fiddler Jim to pour his troubles into other ears, I pushed on towards the Admiral's quarters. A knock bringing no response, I pushed open the door, to find Morgan lying upon his back, snoring most vilely. Yet I had only advanced one pace into the room before he had started up into a sitting position, at the same time swiftly snatching a pistol from under his pillow. When he saw it was only myself and Big Dixon, he put aside his weapon with a chuckle.

"Always best to be on the alert," said he. "Though I can sleep through all the noise out yonder, a stealthy footstep always arouses me. Well, what d'you want, Arthur?"

Whereat I told him the news I had learned from Algernon, namely, that buccaneering was likely soon to be a thing of the past, and that he and his men would soon have to return to peaceful pursuits or run the risk of being outlawed as pirates.

"And d'you think I haven't heard all that, lad?" he asked, his eyes a-twinkle. "I've many a spy to hand me news of that sort."

"But what about your promised march to Panama? Even now it may be too late."

"Not quite, my boy. Though what you have heard about Spain and England making peace may be true enough, the Governor hasn't been officially informed of it yet. Until he is, he'll not attempt to prevent my sailing, I reckon."

"But, sir, the news may come any hour now, and——"

"Tut, we're safe enough for a few days. Just give my bully boys time enough to rid themselves of some of the gold doubloons that are burning holes in their pockets, and we'll be off."

A sudden lull in the noise outside drew Morgan to the door. The silence had been caused by the entry into the rum-shop of a number of sailors, whose smart appearance and neat uniforms contrasted mightily with the assortment of gaudy clothes worn by the buccaneers.

"Ship just in from England, Admiral," volunteered a tall, saturnine-looking fellow standing near us.

"There you see," I whispered, "the message will soon be delivered."

Morgan pulled at his moustache nervously. "Maybe, maybe," he agreed. "The sooner we're off, perhaps, the better. But it's a big undertaking, the march to Panama. There's the Castle of San Lorenzo ought to be taken—it commands the Chagres River, which must be the path we take. Then I must make Santa Catalina the base of supplies. Men I can get, and ships I can get, both in a hurry. But 'twill take several weeks to collect such a store of provisions as we need if we attempt the march."

At this moment, for a second time that evening, a hush fell upon the ruffians that filled the room. An awed whisper ran from one to another, "The witch of the Island! Old Dame Crowfoot!" I had heard of her often enough before, once from Morgan himself, and it was with interest not untinged with fear that I looked upon this old woman, so feared by the superstitious buccaneers.

She was old and bent, and as she hobbled slowly across the room towards us she looked neither to right nor left. Scanty locks of dirty grey escaped from her black hood and hung down on either side of her sallow face. She was clad in a black cloak that enveloped her completely, except where a pair of skinny arms protruded, to enable her claw-like hands to clutch the crook of a sturdy stick upon which she leaned. She halted a few yards in front of Morgan, then slowly lifted her wizened face, and gazed at him fixedly. I was surprised to find such keen, piercing eyes in such a weak, age-bent creature.

"You are worried about the expedition you want to make to Panama, eh?" she asked in a shrill, cracked voice, then laughed mockingly as Morgan's start of surprise showed she had hit the mark.

"Spain and England friends again, where will the buccaneers fill their purses?" and again came the laugh which sent an unpleasant thrill down my spine.

"Don't talk in riddles, Dame Crowfoot. Help us if you can," quoth Morgan testily.

"There you are, there you are!" chanted the old beldame. "You never did have much patience. And you don't believe what Old Dame Crowfoot says, now, do you?"

"Of course I do. Why——"

"Oh, ho! And you didn't tell the boy that stands by your side about my prophecy? 'You'll be deceived by the man you trust most,' was what I said, and you told him you couldn't believe it, because you know Captain Bradley wouldn't cheat you."

The Admiral's expression was sufficient admission of his guilt. She chuckled over his discomfiture for fully a minute, then once again continued her squeaking.

"So you don't value old Dame Crowfoot's warnings. All the same, I'm going to tell you something more. If you want to succeed in your march to Panama, you must sail for Santa Catalina to-morrow!"

"To-morrow? Impossible. And who told you I meant to go to Santa Catalina at all?"

"Ha, ha, Harry Morgan! Old Dame Crowfoot knows all, yes, all. You mean to make Santa Catalina your base, don't you? And you mean to send an expedition to take San Lorenzo Castle. Well, if you want it, send a party at once under Captain Bradley. He's the only man that will do the job well, though there will be black news for you when you hear the castle has fallen."

"But Captain Bradley's not at Port Royal. He's away——"

"He'll be in before dawn, and if you're wise you'll send him fresh men so that he can get away at once. And now listen to me again if you really want to capture Panama. What says the Scripture? 'Take no heed for the morrow.' Mark it well. Don't you go storing up provisions to take with you. Let each man have one good meal before he starts, and carry no food with him. Mark it well. No food to be carried!"

"But that's madness," expostulated Morgan. "How are we to live on the journey? We *must* take food."

"If you do, you'll fail. Has old Dame Crowfoot learned to read the future for her words to be wasted? Look!" With a sudden gesture, surprisingly swift considering her age, she snatched up a glass tumbler from a nearby table. "Now if I dash this to the floor it will smash into atoms, won't it? Ay, that's what you think. But I say it will not even chip. Watch!" With all her force she flung the tumbler to the ground. To my astonishment it remained whole, as she had said it would. I know not how she managed the trick (for trick it must have been), but its effect upon the buccaneers in the tavern was unmistakable.

"Take note of what the old dame says!" "Listen to the witch of Port Royal, Admiral!" "It's tight belts for us, but never mind, so long as we reach Panama!' These, and other expressions, were freely flung about, while Morgan stood staring down at the glass tumbler, not knowing what to say. Meanwhile the old beldame stood looking at him with triumphant eyes, chuckling long and loudly at his bewilderment.

"Well, what is it to be?" she demanded at length, though the triumph in her voice left no doubt as to what answer she expected. "Empty stomachs and the gold of Panama, or of food in plenty and a dismal death in the marshes on the way? 'Tis in your hands, Henry Morgan, to choose for good or ill."

Morgan turned to the buccaneers, and addressed them in the rich, great voice that always compelled attention. "Well, Brethren, you hear what our friend, the witch of Port Royal, has to say. That we ought to start our enterprise quickly is certain. England and Spain are offering each other the palm of friendship. But to attempt the march to Panama without food seems madness."

But the buccaneers heeded not his appeal. Great fists drummed upon the table, cutlass blades were waved excitedly in the air, and rough throats took up the refrain, "Listen to the witch of Port Royal, Morgan. Empty stomachs and sacks of gold!"

"Well, what is it to be?" asked the witch a second time, half turning to go.

Out flashed Morgan's cutlass, and he leaped upon the table, a magnificent figure of a man.

"To Panama!" he cried. "We'll do as Dame Crowfoot bids. To-morrow, if I can get a sober crew aboard my ship, I'm setting sail for Santa Catalina!"

CHAPTER XIV

THE MARCH ACROSS THE ISTHMUS

I EXPECT that in years to come, History will relate how Morgan made Santa Catalina his base for the operations against Panama.

So great was the reputation that Morgan now held, that over two thousand desperadoes enrolled in his service; and under his command he had no fewer than thirty-seven galleons, more than had ever been gathered before in one fleet in those waters.

Following the advice of the witch of Port Royal, he had sent Captain Bradley, with some four hundred men, to subdue the Castle of San Lorenzo. Thither Morgan and his fleet set sail, once his force was made up, and in eight days we sighted the castle.

"It's ours! It's ours!" came the joyful cry from the mast-head. Sure enough, as we all presently saw, the English flag fluttered bravely at the flag-staff of the castle. Great was the jubilation aboard. It was felt that this was a good omen for the success of the expedition.

Our boat was met by a number of Bradley's men (all glad to see us) led by the Spanish spy, Diaz, and a massive, broad-faced fellow called Palabra. This latter seemed to be looked upon by the men ashore as a leader, though as far as I knew he had not even been one of the lower officers when Captain Bradley's expedition had set out.

"Well, you managed things all right," said Morgan, pointing upwards to where the flag of England twisted and writhed in the gusty breeze. "Where's Cap'n Bradley? He's done good work."

There was silence for a brief minute, broken by Palabra.

"I'm sorry to say Cap'n Bradley's dead, sir."

The Admiral started. "Dead?" he repeated.

"Killed, sir, in our assault on the castle."

And he went on to give an account of some of the perils encountered in the march they had made to the landward side of the castle, and the galling fire that had greeted their first assaults.

"It was cruel fighting," concluded Palabra. "When the outer palisade was almost down, Bradley led us in a last charge, but though the garrison had lost dozens of men, they met us with such a fire that we could not face it. It was here that Bradley died, a cannon-ball whipping off his head as cleanly as though he'd been struck with an axe. I carried his body out of the fight, but it was wasted labour, seein' what had happened to him. Before I'd had proper time to put his body to earth, the Dons had quit their shelter, an' charged at us. Their commander it was who inspired them to such a stubborn defence, an' though I tried to get at him, not once could I manage it."

"That's where I came in," cried Diaz cunningly. "I knew that so long as this commander lived the castle would never be ours. Therefore I carefully loaded my musket, an' withdrew somewhat from the fight to a place where I could rest the barrel as I aimed. He was just shoutin', 'Keep the flag of Spain aloft! Keep the flag——!' when I fired.

The bullet struck him in the head, and sank into his brain."

"That was the shot that won us the castle," agreed Palabra. "Their commander down, the survivors gave in. We've been usin' them ever since in re-building the castle."

"And your losses?" inquired Morgan.

"A hundred men or so, at least. But the Dons fared worse. Close on three hundred of them were slain, and thirty we took prisoners. Only eight escaped in all—in a boat we pursued, but could not catch—and they, I take it, will have borne news of what has happened up the Chagres River to Panama."

Morgan said nothing about the number of men lost in taking San Lorenzo, though the casualties were far heavier than he had anticipated. Instead, he turned towards the harbour in which some dozen Spanish galleons lay at anchor.

"How came these here?" he asked.

Palabra gave a grin of self-satisfaction.

"They sailed in, one by one," he explained. "Having taken the castle, I remembered the commander's words, 'Keep the flag of Spain aloft,' and I did so for several days. As a reward nearly every day some Spanish galleon sailed in to lie under the protection of our guns, and they have stayed with us ever since!"

"You have done well, both of you," said Morgan, gazing appreciatively at the fresh vessels at his disposal. "You, Palabra," he went on, "shall be raised to the rank of captain under my command. Choose which of these vessels you would prefer—it shall be yours. You, Diaz, I must confess, I thought to be untrustworthy. You have proved me wrong by the part you have played in taking San Lorenzo. You shall be made a lieutenant in my fleet, and what is more, I appoint you head of the scouting service, for which extra payment will be given. I am greatly pleased with you both!"

At Lorenzo we stayed several weeks. Much as Morgan wanted to be off, there was a great deal of initial preparation to be done. Even though the buccaneers intended following the instructions of the witch of Port Royal in not carrying with them any food, yet there were guns to be taken, and suitable rafts had to be constructed to carry these up the River Chagres. Then the Castle of San Lorenzo itself had been so severely damaged during Captain Bradley's fierce assault that much toil was required to put it into suitable condition. All the prisoners in the buccaneers' hands were set to work on this, and presently fresh trenches were dug, new palisades erected, and platforms laid for guns.

Morgan ordered all the guns carried by the Spanish vessels to be taken ashore, save those of the *Gracias a Dios*, which Palabra had chosen for his command.

Diaz, in his new position as leader of the buccaneers' espionage service, had not been idle. Before San Lorenzo had been completely refortified, he came to Morgan with news that the Spaniards not only anticipated our forthcoming project, but had laid plans to prevent its accomplishment.

"Nearly four thousand Dons alone, to say nothing of their Indian allies, will dispute our progress," declared Diaz. "They're building ambuscades, cunningly concealed, at various points of our journey. It will need all our courage to get to Panama."

"Isn't there any other course we can take?" demanded Morgan.

"No; there's but the one path possible, that which starts by way of the Chagres River. That will be difficult enough, as you'll find, without reckoning the fighting at all. My advice is that we start at once, before the Spaniards have time to build many ambuscades."

It was because of Diaz's remarks that the expedition set off before all had been done that Morgan wished. He garrisoned the reconstructed Castle of San Lorenzo with five hundred men, under the command of Captain Norman. The ships of his fleet he manned with one hundred and fifty of his staunchest fighting men, and the remainder, numbering fourteen hundred buccaneers, were marshalled ready for the great march.

A huge feast was prepared just before the rafts and canoes were unmoored from the banks. The superstitious buccaneers intended to keep strictly to what the witch of Port Royal had said. No food was to be carried on the march! It was absolute madness; boy as I was, I could have told them that. But superstition is a powerful master. Morgan and his fourteen hundred men were to curse the prophecies of the old witch many times before they came in sight of Panama.

One and all ate a hearty meal. All through the night huge fires were kept burning by the men who were to stay behind, and whole beasts were cooked for the departing Brethren. Just before dawn the camp was roused, and the buccaneers set to with a will upon the viands prepared for them.

"A full belly to start with!" roared one of them, as he cut off another huge portion of meat which he proceeded to eat at tremendous speed. "We may have to wait till we're in Panama for our next decent meal."

His comrades followed his advice and example right royally, and though the amount of food prepared had been enormous, little remained by the time that gargantuan meal had been concluded.

So on 18th January 1671 we set off on that wonderful march that I believe will be talked about for hundreds of years to come. It would be impossible to describe my feelings as the first raft was unmoored. Had I been merely one of the members of the expedition, with a share of the gold of Panama my aim, I still should have been keyed-up with excitement. For me the occasion was far more important. If only we could accomplish the tremendous task (and I would not admit to myself the possibility of failure) it would be in my power to release my father from imprisonment. No wonder my heart beat high as we at last set out upon that glorious adventure.

And now I find myself in a quandary. The chief purpose of my tale is to tell of my personal adventures in my endeavours to seek out my father's place of captivity, and release him. Yet remembrance of that great march tempts me greatly to describe the journey in full. To do so would mean writing many pages, for there is matter enough and to spare for a dozen books. And so I curb the temptation, and instead put in certain leaves from a diary I kept while that march was in progress.

The leaves of that diary are dirty and torn. In many places the words are quite obliterated. No wonder! Well I recall the difficulties under which I wrote—sometimes by the light of a smoky fire, sometimes in the fierce heat of the noon sun, sometimes when the rain poured down in a continuous deluge, as only it can in the Tropics. Hungry, tired, travel-worn, almost despairing, yet I managed to scrawl those pages some time during each day of our travels, and I treasure them with no little pride as evidence of the part I took in one of the most daring and most heroic exploits ever undertaken by desperate men.

Here, then, are the pages of my diary. I have filled up the few gaps that occur where the original words are missing.

18*th January* 1671.

At last on our way to Panama! A day's march nearer to the happy day when I shall be able, God willing, to set free my father. It has been a hard day. We set off in three divisions. One party marched along the right bank, under Capt. Gentle's command. Knocker commanded the party on the left bank. Morgan's own division went by water—32 canoes and 5 flat-bottomed boats. I was in the first of these boats, along with Dick, Fiddler Jim, and others of the *Rover*. Everybody on the look out for Dons, although Diaz assures us his scouts will give good warning. Every cannon loaded and matches lit, ready for a surprise attack. Nothing occurred, however.

We are now in camp. The men marching ashore grumble greatly. They say the way very difficult, and all sorts of insects and lice burrow into their skin, and suck the blood. Glad I'm in one of the boats. Men beginning to suffer from hunger. One or two have killed small animals, but these not enough for one fraction of the whole force.

Noticed Diaz, Palabra, and Knocker talking secretly. Managed to crawl up near enough to hear some of their conversation. They plan to ferment men's anger against Morgan. Knocker wants to quit buccaneering, and take to piracy on the high seas. Took this information to Morgan, who laughed at me. Said I'm not just to K. because we've not been very good friends in the past. Said he trusted Knocker as much as any man in his force. Could not help reminding him of the words of the witch of Port Royal, namely, that he would be deceived by the one he trusted most.

19*th January*.

We are all beginning to find the pangs of hunger terrible to bear. How foolish of Morgan ever to have taken notice of the mad words of a mad woman! Thank Heaven there is water enough in the fresh streams to quench our thirst.

To-day progress has been slow and painful. Often the water in the river became too shallow for the boats, and sometimes mighty trees fallen across the stream barred our way. On these occasions not only the canoes and boats, but the cannon as well, had to be carried or hauled through the forest till deep water again found.

The toil was bad, the heat and insects worse, the hunger most terrible of all. Morgan addressed the men to-night. He reminded them that the witch of Port Royal had predicted success after mighty suffering. Also he said any day we might encounter ambuscades of the enemy, and having made them retreat, could take any store of food left behind. Knocker said, "Why let the Dons retreat? A few prisoners would be very useful to starving men." By the ferocious look on his face as he said this, I verily believe him to be thinking of turning cannibal.

Much grumbling against Morgan, which I feel sure Knocker and his comrades are encouraging. Tried to listen to conversation as yesterday, but was sent about my business with a tingling ear from Diaz.

20th January.

How we have struggled through the day I cannot say. The heat has been tremendous. As for the pangs of hunger, the following will give some idea of the state in which we find ourselves. Although no sign of the foe as yet, we came upon a deserted ambuscade. Not a trace of food, but some leather bags left. What must some of the buccaneers do but start to fight amongst themselves for possession of these bags! Morgan, backed up by Gentle and some of the *Rover* men, draws pistols and stops the fighting. He had the bags cut up into equal pieces and shared out amongst the men. Some so ravenous they tore at their share like wild beasts. Others soaked the leather in water, beat it between stones, and then roasted it. Tried this way myself, cutting the leather into tiny pieces. Managed to swallow some of them by drinking large draughts of water, but found my hunger but little satisfied.

I am beginning to doubt if we shall ever reach Panama. The Governor of that city has been at great pains to have all food removed from our path. The passage through the forest is well-nigh impossible at times. Great vines grow from trunk to trunk, closing up tracks that once traversed the forest.

Heard Knocker and his cronies plotting this evening. They do not intend injury to Morgan till after he sacks Panama—evidently they think we shall be successful in spite of our difficulties. Once Panama is ours, they will steal all the treasure on which they can lay hands, load it upon the best vessel in the harbour, then sail away and hoist the Skull-and-Crossbones.

21*st January*.

The fourth day of our march over, and our sufferings well-nigh unendurable. Two large ambuscades found to-day—both deserted, and no food in either. More leather bags, but these, though eaten, relieve our hunger but little.

22*nd January*.

At last some food found, but none has passed my lips. Still, it gives hopes of supplies being discovered soon. We reached Barbacaos, but it was quite deserted. At first no supplies whatever could be found, but presently Diaz (who, for all his faults, is a splendid woodsman) found a concealed store of food—some meal, several bunches of bananas, and some wine. Not enough to share out, so Morgan (with much difficulty) gave them to the weakest of the force. Many, in truth, had fainted on the march today.

23*rd January*.

At last I am no longer hungry! It seems incredible that I could have struggled on these six days without any real food, and have endured all the terrible hardships of the way. We came upon a barn full of maize close on noon. The men simply went mad. No stopping to cook the stuff—a wild cramming of the grain into one's mouth. What was left over—little enough—we loaded into knapsacks to carry with us.

The men curse continually, chiefly against the witch of Port Royal, and Morgan himself. Yet Morgan is the only man who could keep them together, and lead them to success.

Hope has come back to me! I think we shall reach Panama after all. What is more, I have a feeling that I shall find my father still alive.

To-day has been full of incidents—some hopeful in character, others disappointing. At last we have actually exchanged shots with the foe. We came suddenly upon an ambuscade of Indians, who fired a flight of arrows upon us. On our replying with a hail of musket-shot, they turned and fled straightway, howling insults. Two men wounded, but not seriously. If the Indians suffered any casualties, they carried them off.

Later in the day we sighted Vera Cruz, or rather smoke rising from the direction where Diaz's spies reported it to lie. On reaching it found only a smouldering ruin. Nothing to eat except dogs and cats. Many of the buccaneers gorged themselves upon these. Hungry though I was, in spite of the maize I had eaten, I managed to refrain from following the example. Fortunately I was not to regret this. Diaz found a store of bread and wine, skilfully hidden, and told Morgan of his find. He was rewarded with a promise of three hundred pieces of eight, and the store was fairly divided amongst us all. It gave a moderate ration apiece, and that is why I was able to open my diary to-day with the joyful sentence, "I am no longer hungry." But I dread to think that I may be again to-morrow.

24th January.

The seventh day of the march! We are certainly nearing Panama, for we encountered Dons to-day. Captain Gentle found a dozen of his men missing, and asking Big Dixon, Fiddler Jim, Polly Flinders, and about a score of others to come back with him to see if they were straggling. He found their dead bodies in one of the tilled fields near Vera Cruz. Some had bullets in them, others arrows. As we stood sorrowing, there came a force of about fifty, Spaniards and Indians mixed, who, with loud threats, came bearing down upon us. Angry at the loss of his men, Gentle did not wait for their attack, but charged at them, roaring mightily. Whereupon we followed him, being desperate men. For two or three minutes the issue hung in the balance, but our fury alarmed our assailants, who broke and fled, leaving five of their number behind. Gentle called us off from pursuing, and hurriedly led us in chase of the main body, fearing an encounter with another stronger band.

Morgan has given strict orders against straggling. He says we are now only twenty-five miles from Panama, and that our only chance of success is to keep together. He is not sure that the Dons have not lured him on so that he cannot retreat, in order to wipe out his whole force. If so, dear father, I shall have failed in my quest.

25th January.

I write to-night under tremendous difficulties. Rain is pouring down in a constant deluge. Our plight is indeed pitiable. Hungry, tired, ragged, we cannot sleep because of the downpour. Our fires are all out; we are drenched to the skin. Every effort is being made to keep the powder dry by hiding it in hollows of trees, and wherever there is shelter, but I know not if we shall be successful.

I have found the best shelter I could, underneath a tree which slants, so forming a partial covering. Every now and again, despite my care, splashes fall upon my paper, smudging the writing. . . .

We are at the foot of a hill. To-morrow, Morgan promises, when we climb this hill, we shall see across to the water of the Pacific Ocean, which washes the coast where stands Panama itself!

To-day disaster nearly overtook our army. Morgan himself came within an ace of being slain. We were marching along, through the forest when they fell on us, as though from nowhere, a heavy shower of arrows which struck down close on a score of our men. "Come on, English dogs!" came shots from around us. "Wait till you reach the Savanna! Worse than this awaits you."

The numbers of our assailants we knew not. Morgan, like the fearless lion he is, charged straight at the place from which the arrows had come. Just one instant's hesitation, and the rest of the buccaneers were after him, Dixon and myself close at his heels. Few of the Indians in ambush awaited our coming; but one stepped out as Morgan dashed by his shelter, seized the Admiral by the neck, and struck down at him with a knife. I flung myself on the Indian's shoulders in time to upset his aim, and was flung rudely to the ground for my pains. Dixon, however, was on the alert, and sent the Indian crashing with a terrific blow.

Nothing eatable found all day. Knocker urged that the bodies of the slain Indians should be eaten! Few would support him, and so his beastly suggestion was not carried out. Morgan urged the need for speed, so we pushed on as fast as we could.

How I wish the rain would stop! How I wish I had something to eat!

26th January.

What a day! I write by the light of a huge fire, over which a whole beast is roasting. The buccaneers are nearly mad with excitement. They seem to have no idea of our desperate situation. From the darkness around, insults are being hurled at us from Spaniards who have ridden out from Panama. Apart from firing an occasional musket as a warning, the buccaneers take no heed. Thrice a cannon-ball has hummed towards us from Panama. Each has fallen short; the firing is ominous as a sign of the warm reception awaiting us.

We ascended the hill at early dawn—Buccaneers' Hill, Knocker has dubbed it. As we reached the top I cried aloud my joy and wonder. In the distance, calm and peaceful, lay the blue waters of the Pacific Ocean. On it, their white sails glistening in the early sunshine, were ships of all kinds, promising a rich spoil if ever Panama fell into our hands. And below us, stretching towards the forest which hid the City of Gold from our view, was mile upon mile of green savanna. What gladdened our hearts (once we had become used to the grand prospect opened before our eyes) were the many herds of animals that could be seen on the plain below.

At the sight of these beasts our hunger became overpowering. Led by Knocker, Diaz, and Palabra, the buccaneers drew their blades, and with wild cries and yells down the hill they dashed towards the savanna. Morgan at first attempted to check their ferocious rush, but soon desisted, seeing how useless his efforts were. As the buccaneers drew near to the grazing cattle, these turned hither and thither, not knowing where to run. In amongst the cattle plunged the buccaneers, who split up into small bands, each party singling out an animal for destruction. It was pitiful to see them cut down the frightened beasts, and immediately hack off the still-warm flesh, and eat it, raw, with teeth gleaming like wild tigers snarling over their prey.

It was almost dark when the savanna was reached, and so the sudden fall of darkness did not end the feast. Some are eating now, as though to make up in one meal for the weary days of hunger.

I myself waited until some meat was roasted before eating, and even then, hungry though I was, I ate but sparingly, knowing it dangerous for a famished person to overload his stomach. Through this I have been spared the bouts of sickness many of the buccaneers have suffered.

Warm am I and well fed, yet my heart is low within me. How can this much-diminished band of ragged, travel-worn men, despite the desperate courage of the buccaneers, ever defeat the powerful army that Diaz's spies report has been drawn up to bar our approach? Yet retreat, without stores, through the trackless forest, is unthinkable.

27th January.

At last we are within sight of Panama! Tomorrow I shall know whether all my efforts have been vain. Between us and the city is encamped a mighty host of Spaniards. As I look around at my comrades, whose faces no less than their clothes bear testimony to the sufferings they have endured, I fear that naught but disaster can overtake us.

To-day we started off at dawn, in fine fettle, flags waving, drums rolling, trumpets blaring, and every one on tiptoe with eager expectation. Many of the officers (Morgan himself among them) had managed to capture horses, and now bestrode them. Very different was our way from the rotting odorous forest through which we had so lately plunged. Here in many parts the land is under cultivation. Orange groves, lemon and fig trees are mingled with bananas, palms, and the like.

Diaz, who had been out with his scouts before dawn, suddenly appeared at the head of our procession. He brought news that the route we were following was impassable. Every clump of trees, every scrap of cover along the road we were following were lined with musketeers, while in places big guns had been brought from Panama, and trained so as to bear upon us as we approached.

Morgan asked Diaz what he proposed. The scout answered that our best plan would be to swing round to the westward, plunge once more into a forest, and approach Panama from quite another direction. Morgan was at first dubious as to the wisdom of following this advice, until Diaz pointed out that as this route was so difficult, the Dons would never have thought of guarding it.

So it turned out. Though the way was rough, we found our progress unopposed, and late in the afternoon again emerged on to the savanna, to find a range of low hills between ourselves and the city of our quest. Less than two miles brought us to these, and before the sun sank, we had reached the summit of one of them.

Before us, at last, lay Panama. What a shout broke from the throats of our men as they beheld the beautiful houses of the city, with the grand tower of the cathedral dominating all else!

"At last," murmured Morgan, rubbing his hands, and I knew that he had an ambition to fulfil every whit as dear to him as mine was to me. His was the desire to sack this city of gold.

But presently our eyes turned from the city to the force which blackened the plain before us. Already an army so large had mustered that to me it looked madness ever to think of opposing it.

Morgan decided to leave offering battle till

the morrow. We are resting here for the night and as I write I can hear the insults shouted at us from a troop of Spanish horsemen who hover just beyond musket-shot.

To-morrow all will be decided. Father, father, pray Heaven it will be within my power to visit your prison and release you!

CHAPTER XV

THE BATTLE BEFORE PANAMA

AND now I abandon my diary, since once again I become one of the principal actors in the story I set out to tell.

Dawn broke, to find the buccaneers already under arms. As I looked round upon their dare-devil features, I marvelled at the courage that still filled these men. The days of hunger and torture had done little, so far as I could judge, to quell their spirit.

Morgan called me to him to know if I had seen Diaz. Within a few minutes I found him, and conducted him to where Morgan stood.

"Well, what news?" asked the Admiral, and it astonished me to see the anxiety with which he waited the response. The danger must indeed be great, thought I, if Morgan himself has fears as to the outcome of the day's battle.

"The news is none too good, but might be worse. Our quick march has given the Dons scant time to prepare for our coming, yet there is a force far outnumbering our own between here and the city."

"Do you know their numbers?" asked Morgan.

"Fairly well. I should put their foot at about three thousand, perhaps a hundred or so less. That doesn't include the townspeople, though—but, anyway, they don't count for much."

"Any cavalry?"

"Ay! Four hundred picked men. And besides that, the Dons intend using a fresh force against us. Bulls! They've herds numbering two thousand bulls in all, and a hundred Indians employed to drive them full-tilt into our ranks."

"H'm!" said Morgan. "Forewarned is forearmed. I fancy buccaneers will know how to deal with cattle, seeing that it was our trade before the Spaniards drove us to the sea. All the same, the odds against us are great. We've scarcely twelve hundred men left; two hundred lost on the march, mark you. Still, there's no drawing back now, even if we wished."

He now proceeded to array his force. He himself, taking about five hundred men, was to command the right wing. Knocker, with an equal force, was in charge of the left wing. Captain Gentle, who bore the reputation of being one of the finest shots in the ranks of the buccaneers was given instructions to choose two hundred picked marksmen, and to use them to the best advantage, according to the tactics of the enemy.

The leaders lost no time in forming up our men in the stations they were to occupy, for scouts, whom Diaz had posted upon neighbouring hills, signalled frantic messages that the Dons were coming in our direction at full speed. Their cavalry arrived first, and of a sudden the air was filled with cries of "Vive el Rey! Vive el Rey!" and down the sloping side of the hill before us swept the Spanish horse.

A splendid sight they made. The sun's rays lit up their polished accoutrements, and flashed upon the horsemen's swords, which they waved threateningly as they came. The horses were gallant animals, legs stretched out to fullest extent as they galloped, and they appeared to vie with one another as to which would bear its rider against our ranks the sooner.

"What chance shall we have against them?" grumbled one of the buccaneers, loud enough for Morgan to hear. "A pretty sight our horsemen look against theirs," and he pointed in derision to an ass one of the captains was riding, an animal which had been captured upon the savanna.

Morgan had swung himself off his horse in a trice, and clapped a pistol against the man's head.

"Another cowardly word from you, and you die!" he cried so ferociously that the man began to stammer excuses. "As for the rest of you," went on Morgan, addressing the men with flashing eyes, "don't forget the deeds we've done together in days now past. Fight, my lads, as we've fought together before. Don't be misled by any croaker like this."

For answer a wild cheer rang from out the husky throats of the buccaneers, and each gripped his weapon with more resolution and hope than before. No wonder, for Morgan's voice carried such conviction that I, for one, lost all fear of defeat.

Meanwhile the charging cavalry had been checked. Between them and ourselves stretched a swamp, into which the horses had plunged, and here they were only able to move with difficulty. Whilst they were in this plight, Captain Gentle, who had led his picked marksmen to a point of vantage upon a neighbouring hill, instructed his men to fire over our heads at the bemired cavalry.

So accurate was the fire that very soon the Spaniards' ranks began to give evidence of confusion, and many a horse fell to be trampled upon by the hooves of the other animals, and many a saddle was emptied of its dashing rider.

"See!" cried Morgan, pointing to the struggling horsemen, "already we are showing our power. Here, boy, slip over to Palabra and tell him to take a hundred men against the Dons' cavalry. If he can destroy them, I'll give him double his share of the loot."

Palabra was not at all loth to advance, especially when he heard the reward likely to be his. His men followed his lead with alacrity; but before his force was within two hundred yards of the cavalry, the leading horsemen had struggled through the marshy ground, and were forming ranks to charge once more. Palabra thereupon altered his plans, and led his men by a circuitous route through the marsh, and interposed his force between the Spanish cavalry and foot-soldiers, so cutting off the former's retreat.

Looking backwards (for I had kept with Palabra's force) I saw the re-formed ranks of cavalry sweep down upon Morgan's men. The buccaneers greeted their advance with volley upon volley of accurate musket-fire, and with a thrill of joy I saw the ranks of horsemen become perceptibly thinner. Just as the Admiral's force moved forward, however, to engage the enemy in hand-to-hand conflict, a sudden warning cry from one of my own party drew my attention to a danger that was threatening us.

Apparently the Dons thought the time ripe for sending against us the huge herd of bulls designed to fling our ranks in confusion. I turned to see a black, seething mass moving rapidly in our direction, urged on by the shrill, piercing cries of the Indian drovers. My first impulse was to turn and run. To my surprise, I found the remainder of Palabra's men quite unperturbed, even a little scornful at the Spaniards' lack of knowledge in thus attempting to destroy them.

"Hardly a man of us," quoth Palabra contemptuously, "who was not once a hunter of wild cattle, and they think to frighten us with a herd of bulls."

At a given signal the buccaneers dropped to knee, and a combined volley of musket-shot was sent into the charging herd. Most of the leading bulls were shot down, so impeding the paths of those behind. The unexpected volley so terrified the remaining bulls that they turned hither and thither in a wild effort to avoid the terrible danger in front of them. Consequently the beasts stampeded in every direction save where they were meant to charge. The Indian drivers were quickly overturned, and smashed to a pulp by the beating hooves, and very soon a part of the herd was plunging in amongst the Spanish soldiery, causing no little destruction and confusion.

Palabra sent me back to the Admiral with news of what had happened. I found Morgan rallying his men to beat off another cavalry charge. Conspicuous amongst the ranks of the Spaniards was a richly-dressed officer who bestrode a magnificent black stallion. He was riding up and down in front of his force, apparently urging on his men to fresh deeds of heroism, for ever and again he waved his sword to where our triple ranks awaited the charge.

"Aim for that officer," cried Morgan to some of his best marksmen. "While he lives their cavalry will be unbroken."

And now the Spanish officer set himself in front of his men, and flashed his sword over his head, so that the polished blade sparkled white in the rays of the sun. There followed the thunder of hooves as the squadron charged full-tilt towards us, mingled with the full-throated cries of the riders as they strove alike to encourage themselves and strike terror in our hearts. It was magnificent to watch—the powerful great horses, urged to topmost speed; the jingling of bridles, and clatter of accoutrement; the battle-distorted faces of the riders; and above all, the splendid picture of their leader, as he rode in front of his troopers.

"Fire!" cried Morgan, while yet their front rank was fifty paces away. A sheet of flame and smoke burst from the muskets of our front rank, who were lying prone upon the ground. Still the Spanish officer rode unharmed, though a ball had whisked his helmet from his head. "Fire!" cried Morgan again, and the muskets of the men in the second rank, who were kneeling each upon one knee, spoke in unison. "Does he bear a charmed life?" muttered the Admiral, as it was seen that the black stallion and its rider came on at unchecked speed. By now the said officer was almost touching our musket barrels. "Fire!" cried Morgan, for the third time. With a loud roar the muskets of the third rank were discharged, and simultaneously the daring officer reined his horse so that it reared high upon its hind legs. When the smoke had disappeared, it was seen that the black stallion had fallen, and was threshing about in its death agony. But its rider had thrown himself clear, and was leading the charge upon foot.

There followed terrible minutes of confused madness. Great horses loomed overhead. Swords flashed. Pistols cracked. Men yelled and groaned.

Of a sudden I found myself face to face with the Spanish officer who had so gallantly led his men. A sabre cut across his forehead gleamed red and ugly. His sword was snapped in twain. A big patch of red stained his uniform just under his heart. In spite of his wounds he was still upon his feet, urging on his men.

I raised my pistol to shoot him. "Ah! would you?" he hissed, and struck my weapon with his broken sword, dashing it from my hand. He raised the jagged blade to strike me down.

A great horse, snorting with fright or pain, reared itself suddenly above him, pawing with maddened hooves. His skull was smashed by its wild lashing, and he fell, never to move again.

The turmoil continued. I felt that all hope of escape was over; that the din, the fury, the confusion would last for ever. There came a sudden lull, like the dropping of the wind in the midst of a furious gale.

Half stunned, I looked about me. Buccaneers, horses, and Spaniards lay in heaps upon the ground. Other buccaneers, still living, bound their wounds. Some, even, reloaded their muskets to fire at the retreating foe. Those horsemen that still survived were seeking safety in flight, galloping furiously in all directions, though most were headed for Panama.

"Thank Heaven!" cried Morgan. "Their

cavalry is broken. Now we have a chance of taking Panama."

I gave him Palabra's message, and Morgan determined to march at once against the Spanish infantry. Worn out though his men were by recent furious fighting (for the charge I had helped to beat back was the sixth against the right wing), there was no opportunity for rest. The ranks of the buccaneers were quickly formed, and Morgan led them, at the double, to where Palabra's men were engaged in a musketry duel with a force twenty times more numerous.

Very foolishly the Dons did not force their attack, so as to meet us hand to hand, when their superior numbers would have decided the issue. Instead, they continued to exchange volleys of musket-shot, and mighty poor marksmen they were. Our men, on the contrary, did great execution every time they fired. It was almost a massacre, for dozens of the Dons dropped each time we fired a volley.

"It is time to finish the matter!" said Morgan, as he gazed keenly at the fast-diminishing ranks of his opponents. "Take this message to Knocker. Tell him to move with his men round the Spaniards' right flank, so as to take them in the rear. Directly he attacks, I will lead my men forward to help him."

Knocker grumbled on receiving the message, complaining that he and his men were expected to bear the brunt of the fighting, while Morgan and his cronies had a giant's share of any spoil taken. He said this loudly enough for many of his malcontents to hear, and when they openly sympathised with him, and asked him how long he intended to be treated so shabbily, I realised how many adherents Knocker and his two fellow-conspirators were gaining. Yet in spite of his grumbling, Knocker obeyed instructions promptly enough, and began to lead his men through the morass while I hurriedly rejoined Morgan.

The final attack was never made. Before Knocker could reach firm land, the Spaniards, disheartened by their heavy losses, suddenly fled in complete disarray. Most of the fugitives flung down their muskets, and any other baggage that might impede their flight, and set off at full speed. Morgan's buccaneers jumped to their feet in delight at the spectacle, and fired at the flying soldiers so long as they were within range; but no attempt was made to follow. Hardened though the buccaneers were, the strain of their recent privations had tested their endurance to the utmost, and the morning's heavy fighting had left them too weak to pursue. Once the Dons were out of sight, the Brethren flung themselves to the ground, and rested their tired limbs for many hours.

Early in the afternoon Morgan mustered his men, and the roll was called. Considering the desperate nature of the fighting, his losses were small—about two hundred men—though his force was so scanty that he could ill afford to lose any. The Dons' losses were three or four times as heavy, and besides that a number of prisoners had fallen into our hands.

You may be sure that I soon questioned these prisoners for news of my father. One or two pretended to have knowledge of his whereabouts, but on further questioning I found they were lying, probably hoping thereby to win freedom.

I was almost in despair of learning any reliable news when Big Dixon, whom I had not seen since I first joined Palabra's force early in the battle, came excitedly up to me.

"Thank Heaven you're safe, boy! Morgan would not let me keep with you to-day—said I was too valuable a fighter to be allowed to act as a nurse-maid. I've had some one else to protect instead—your old friend Algy."

"Is he safe?" I asked eagerly.

"Yes, but wishing he'd never been born. He swears the mosquitoes have taken a special liking to him. He thinks a lot of you, Arthur, you know, and I can't help admiring him for joining this expedition to help you if he can."

"Yes," I agreed; "he's proved himself a man. And how's Fiddler Jim, Polly, and the rest?"

"Two of the *Rover's* men slain, poor lads, but those you mention are well enough, save for slight scratches. But that's not what I came to tell you. D'you know whom I've just seen?"

It was useless to guess, so I begged him to tell me.

"D'you remember the Spaniard who first gave you real news of your father? The man we took at Porto Bello, I mean. Said he was son of your father's gaoler, if I remember rightly."

"Do you mean the man to whom I gave a message for my father, in case he might find him at Panama?"

"That's the man," agreed Big Dixon. "Well, I've just seen him. He's in Knocker's hands, along with three priests. The buccaneers are torturing the priests, I believe."

"We must hurry and find the youth," said I,

"lest perhaps Knocker kills him. He's not the one to keep prisoners if there's no profit to be gained from them. Perhaps this youth delivered the message I sent by him perhaps he may even have an answer."

Big Dixon curbed my impatience. "Don't let Knocker know you are interested in his prisoners," he advised, "or it's most likely he'll dispose of them just to spite you."

There was enough truth in this to make me determined to proceed warily. I was helped to seek out the prisoner by Morgan ordering me to summon Knocker to his presence. Swiftly I ran with the message, breaking in on the captain whilst he was still questioning a priest while his other prisoners stood in a frightened group near-by. With a throb of joy I saw the youth still unharmed.

". . . treasure of the cathedral," came the tail-end of the priest's words, as I entered. On seeing me, Knocker scowled, and curtly bade his informant cease.

I gave him Morgan's message, and he ordered me to follow him, leaving his prisoners guarded by some of his special followers. On the way to Morgan, however, I managed to give the captain the slip, and hastened back to where the prisoners lay bound. As I approached I availed myself of every scrap of cover I could find, and found the guards were casting dice. Thanks to their attention being thus engaged, I was able, by dint of slow creeping forward upon my stomach, to worm alongside the gaoler's son unperceived by any of the buccaneers.

Stealthily I nudged him, and in surprise he turned over to face me. At first he did not recognise me, but presently recollection dawned in his eyes. I brusquely clapped my hand upon his mouth as he opened it to speak.

"Careful," I whispered. "Speak softly, or we shall be overheard."

Thereupon, with tears in his eyes, he begged me to help him escape. But though I felt sorry for the man, I had not sought him out just to assist him.

"Do you remember?" I asked. "You were going to seek out my father, and deliver a message to him."

"I did, Señor, I did. Your father——"

"Is he alive and well?" I asked so eagerly that it was the turn of the Spanish youth to remind me that caution was necessary. "Yes, alive, and fairly well," he assured me. "Even now he rests in a dungeon in Panama—that is, unless they kill him when the buccaneers attack the city."

The thought sent a cold shiver all over me. "Is it likely?" I demanded.

The youth nodded gloomily. "Very likely, Señor, for my countrymen are both angry and alarmed at the buccaneer's daring. Already some of the prisoners have been executed."

I felt stunned. Had I, after such perils and hardships, come within arm's length, as it were, of my father, only to find him slain just before I could release him? "Never," I whispered fiercely. "Somehow or other he must be released."

"Why not disguise yourself as a Spaniard?" suggested the youth. "Help me to escape, and I'll help you enter Panama. Once there, it might easily be arranged to release your father."

Hope flooded back within me. "The very thing!" I said. "Swear you'll not betray me, and I'll help you escape straightway."

"By the Holy Saints, I swear it," he said solemnly; whereat I drew my knife and cut his bonds asunder.

CHAPTER XVI

HOW I ENTERED THE CITY

I LAY still, while Miguel (as my new comrade was called) chafed his numbed limbs. Directly he felt the blood coursing through them once more, I signalled to him to follow me.

On hands and knees (sometimes upon stomachs) we wormed our way cautiously beyond the ken of our gambling guards. Once at a safe distance, I left Miguel, bidding him cast off his Spanish garments while I hunted around the bodies of slain buccaneers, despoiling them of their apparel.

Presently he was arrayed to my satisfaction, and I bade him follow me boldly wherever I went. "But answer not if any of the Brethren speak to you," I warned him. "I'll do any talking necessary."

Miguel, despite a natural nervousness, played his part well, walking along with a swaggering air as though a buccaneer in real truth. My first business was to seek out Big Dixon and tell him what I proposed. Then, with such of my comrades as would accompany me, would come the daring project of entering Panama.

Big Dixon, loyal as ever, though he knew full well the risky nature of the adventure, readily agreed to join me. "If we don't save your father, 'twill not be for want of effort," said he. "It's good news, Arthur, to hear that Sir Hugh is still alive."

At his suggestion, Miguel and I set out at

once. "The longer he hangs around the camp here, the greater the chance of someone discovering he's a Don. Wait for the rest of us over by yonder grove," and he pointed to a clump of trees about a mile distant.

Thither Miguel and I repaired, and as we went I learned all I could about my father's condition. That he was weak from long imprisonment was only to be expected. To my joy I found that he had not yet been tortured by the Inquisition, and that he kept cheerful and hopeful in spirits. "Your message to him, Señor, was almost as great a joy to him as release from his dungeon would have been," Miguel declared. "When first I knew him, his chief worry was concerning yourself, whether or not you had escaped."

We did not waste our time while awaiting Big Dixon's arrival. Dead Spaniards lay about in plenty, and we made a selection of their clothes, helmets, and weapons, ready to disguise our comrades when they should come up. Our skins were so bronzed by the tropical sun that there was little difference between our colour and the swarthiness common to Spaniards. When I had put on the clothing belonging to one of the Spanish infantry who had fallen—choosing from one of small stature as being likely to fit—I swear that a very creditable Don I made, though the clothes were somewhat heavy and burdensome after the freedom of living in open shirt and no jacket among the buccaneers.

Big Dixon and his party arrived well within the hour. It included Fiddler Jim, Polly Flinders, the rest of the *Rover* men, and Algy. I tried hard to persuade the latter to abandon the risky adventure, but he persisted in joining us.

Of our party, only two were without a fairly fluent smattering of the Spanish tongue. It was at first thought best to leave these out of the adventure, but so keen were they that we resolved to risk them being discovered through the dumbness they would have to assume. In any case, we might need every man we could get if we became involved in fighting.

"There will be no need for them to talk," said Dixon. "Tie rough bandages round their heads, and pretend they've been shot during the battle."

As we journeyed onward towards Panama we were joined *en route* by real Spaniards who had escaped into the woods and were now returning to Panama to assist in its defence. These eagerly asked questions as to our adventures in the day's fighting, and as eagerly told of their own heroic deeds, narrow escapes, and where they had hidden during their flight. We concocted a plausible tale as to our own part in the battle, but did as much listening as possible lest an incautious remark might cast suspicion upon us.

"They're devils, naught else!" cried a stout little man vehemently. "I'm a peaceful citizen of Panama, I am. Why should I be forced to come out and risk my life and limbs against such demons? Holy Church should excommunicate them."

"A lot of good that would do," chimed in a tall, burly soldier. "As for you having to fight," he added, with all the contempt of a veteran for soft-bodied citizens, "you'll have to fight again soon, or you'll lose your fortune to Morgan and his men, when they come battering at the gate of Panama. That'll hurt you almost as much as losing life or limb, eh, my fine fellow?"

The plump citizen, wishing to avert the scorn thus poured upon him, turned to one of the *Rover's* men with the bandaged jaws and asked him the nature of his wound. The man addressed replied with a grunt, whereupon Miguel, to my great relief (as it proved he intended being loyal) explained that a musket-ball had pierced the wounded man's cheek. "I was next him when he fell," said he. "Clean through the right cheek and out through the left cheek! It nearly struck down two men instead of one, for it whisked past my nose with the buzz of an angry bee."

Nearer and nearer came Panama. And ever my heart beat more quickly within me, and my nerves became more taut.

Yet there was no real danger in entering the town. Fugitives were streaming in from all directions, and every man was welcomed as an extra defender. All unwounded men were at once put to work, preparing the town in readiness for Morgan's final assault. In spite of their heavy defeat of the morning, the citizens of Panama had no intention of yielding their rich city without fighting hard to save it.

At first we joined the other workers, dragging guns into position, building earthworks and barricades, and knocking loopholes in the walls of houses lining the main streets, until our bodies reeked with sweat, and our limbs tired with the strain. Yet for a long time there was no chance of escape. A short, hook-nosed Spaniard, in charge of the preparations, jumped here, there, and everywhere, and let but a man pause to mop his brow, there would follow a sharp reproof, often in the form of a sarcastic question, "D'you think *that* will keep back the Brethren of the Coast?"

Altogether we toiled until eight brass demi-cannon had been well mounted and protected, and laid with their muzzles pointing outwards along the route from which the buccaneers would appear.

Nearly an hour must have passed before we managed to escape the keen eyes of our task-master. Then, the gate having been fortified to his satisfaction, he set a guard upon it, and divided the rest of us into gangs to dig trenches in various parts of the city. Miguel, Big Dixon and I were in the same gang, together with others of our English band, and as the different parties moved off, it was quite easy for us to detach ourselves from the Spaniards and scurry into cover down a side street. Here we were quickly joined by our other comrades, and we rested for a few minutes before laying our plans for the real purpose of our journey to the city.

"The dungeon where your father is kept," said Miguel, "lies in the shadow of the great cathedral. Two men share the duty of guarding the prisoners—my father, and a man we call Pedro the Hairy."

I saw Big Dixon's frame stiffen as he heard the name of the Spaniard he had fought in the camp of the fugitives outside Gibraltar. I could guess his thought. If the ruffianly Spaniard should see him, recognition would almost certainly follow, and without a doubt Pedro would be only too pleased to denounce one who had succeeded in overcoming him.

"Who will be on duty at this time?" I asked.

"Who can say, Señor? The coming of the buccaneers has interfered with all the normal working of the city. But I should think that my father, being old, would be kept there. Pedro, I expect, would have had to march out with our army to the savanna yestere'en."

"Let us, at any rate, make our way towards the prison," I suggested. "Then you, Miguel, if you will, can go on alone and find out who is in charge, and how many men he has with him. We can then arrange our plans accordingly."

This Miguel faithfully promised to do, and we proceeded towards the cathedral quite openly, trusting to our disguise to carry us through without question. Then, and whilst Miguel continued towards the prison, the rest of us spread out, and began to work with pick and shovel, as though marking out the site of fresh trenches to be dug in the very precincts of the cathedral.

As we worked, or pretended to do so, I could not help gazing up in awe and admiration at the beautiful edifice that was rightly called the Wonder of the New World. My thoughts were interrupted by a train of men issuing from the main door of the cathedral, bearing steel-bound chests, which were placed on the ground outside. Presently a score or so of mules were driven up, and the chests loaded upon their patient backs.

"Morgan and his men have spread fear throughout the city," said Dixon. "The churchmen are taking their treasure away, probably to stow it aboard some ship in the harbour. If the buccaneers succeed in taking this place, I'll warrant the treasure is carried across the waters to Spain."

Before the whole of the treasure had been loaded upon the mules, Miguel returned, looking quite happy. "My father only remains," said he. "Pedro the Hairy and the other guards have been called away to help in the defence of the city."

"Have you told your father?" I began, but he interrupted me sharply.

"My father would never consent to any prisoner escaping. You must overcome him and take the keys. But, Señors, I beg you to remember he is an old man, and even though he may show fight, deal as gently with him as you can."

This we readily promised, and followed our guide to a stone building, the door of which was of stout mahogany.

"My father has not seen me," explained Miguel. "I did not want him to know I have had any hand in the rescue of the prisoners—for I suppose you want to release any other English here. I will lead you to the room where my father is sitting."

We slipped inside the stone building, quickly drawing the stout door behind us. We found ourselves in a low-roofed corridor. Miguel led the way, the rest of us following on tiptoe, and presently halted outside a door on our left.

"My father sits within," whispered Miguel. "You may see him if you peer through the keyhole."

There he was right enough, seated in a tall chair which he had tilted backwards until it rested against the edge of a stoutly-built table. The old man was fast asleep, his mouth open, and I could hear the rumble of his snoring.

I whispered to Big Dixon to be ready, and quietly opened the door. My comrade entered on tiptoe, eager to overcome the old gaoler as gently and quickly as possible. But our caution was of no avail. Of a sudden the old man sprang up, as though a nightmare had disturbed his slumbers, and seeing us confronting him he let out a wild yell of alarm, that to my anxious ears appeared loud enough to reach the ears of every one in Panama.

There was no time for delay. With a quick bound Dixon was by the old man's side, his great hand spread over the shrieking mouth, abruptly checking its cry. Polly Flinders at the same time seized the gaoler's wrists and tied them up behind. Very quickly the old man was trussed and gagged; yet for all our speed he suffered no more than could be helped, for we remembered Miguel's plea.

"I wonder if any one heard——" I began, and as if in answer there came the sound of running feet along the stone corridor. Big Dixon and I simultaneously sprang to the doorway, but already the Spanish soldier running up had been seized by our comrades. Miguel, meanwhile, had disappeared.

"Bring him in," said I, and the soldier was brought into the gaoler's room and bound securely. Big Dixon took down from a nail in the wall a bunch of large keys, three of which showed signs of recent use.

As we left the room, Miguel again appeared, having hidden because of the Spanish soldier's appearance. "I have no wish to be called a traitor," he explained. He led us to one of the dungeons in which the English prisoners were kept, handed me a lantern, and allowed me to enter.

Four men were there, lying inertly upon the filthy floor. Quickly I knelt by each in turn, and recognised them as survivors from the *Rover*, but to my sorrow found my father was not one of them.

"It is strange," said Miguel. "He was here two days ago."

"Pedro the Hairy took him away yesterday," explained one of the prisoners when I questioned him. "He hated your father, lad, because he could never break his courage."

Leaving the poor fellows to be cared for by some of our party, Miguel, Big Dixon, Algy, and myself pushed on to a second dungeon. As we opened the door, the stench from within was terrible, but I took little heed of that, hoping to find my father there, but again I was disappointed. More of the *Rover's* crew were there (many of them in a sad plight, poor fellows!), but no sign of my father.

"Quick, Miguel," said I. "Lead on to the next dungeon."

"Alas, Señor," he replied, and his voice chilled me like the breath of death, "all the English prisoners were kept in these two dungeons."

My heart stopped beating, and for a moment my senses swam. Like words spoken from afar off came Big Dixon's voice. "There's a third key that seems to have been used lately. What's it for?"

"Perhaps for the dungeon of death," said Miguel, "though I can never remember any one being flung there. 'Tis deep down and loathsome. Yet, maybe——"

"Lead me there," I interrupted. "We must make sure."

I will not attempt to describe my mingled feelings as Miguel thrust the great key into the lock of the low, forbidding door. Hope and despair struggled for mastery within me. As the door opened inwards, creaking mournfully upon its hinges, the others stood by to let me enter first. For a moment I hesitated, peering into the blackness within, fearing to enter lest the disappointment of not finding my father might break down my courage. Then, holding the lamp aloft, I went in.

At the far end of the dungeon, I espied a dim figure. It was erect against the wall, and as I looked more nearly, I found it was a man, thin and emaciated, naked except for a dirty loincloth, and manacled by hands and feet to iron rings in the wall. A thin, haggard, bearded face turned towards me, its eyes blinking at the unwonted light. And then I had dropped my lamp and sprung forward to fling my arms round the poor, wasted form.

I had found my father at last.

How long I embraced him I could not say. Gone were all thoughts of danger, all memories of the march across the Isthmus, all remembrance that at any moment the guns of Panama might be roaring their defiance at the advancing buccaneers.

It was Big Dixon recalled me to my senses.

"We must waste no time," said he. "We must seek a hiding-place without delay."

Miguel came forward with a suggestion. "There is a passage from here to the cathedral," he said. "There you may find a hiding-place until Panama has fallen, unless the buccaneers are driven back."

"And you?" I asked.

"If possible, my father and I will get aboard one of the galleons in the harbour that wait ready to sail for Spain if the buccaneers take the city. If not, we must take our chance with our countrymen."

My father having been released, he was carried in Big Dixon's stalwart arms, being too weak to

fell, rose and fell, like the beating of a hundred drums. Even yells of rage, and the loud cheers of charging men, were borne dimly to our ears.

In a moment our presence had been forgotten by our pursuers. One of them uttered a brisk command, whereat the rest fell into files, turned to the right, and doubled briskly from the cathedral door. Before they left, the heavy reports of the Spaniards' demi-cannon again boomed out, making the coloured windows rattle at the roar.

"Saved, at least for the time," whispered my father.

"Ay!" agreed Dixon, listening intently. "Morgan is making his final bid for Panama!"

CHAPTER XVII

THE FALL OF PANAMA

WHILE the guns of the defenders thundered defiance and the musketry of each side told of the fierceness of the struggle, we were left to consider what would be best for us to do. After a hurried consultation we decided to remain within the shelter of the cathedral walls until we knew what success had attended the buccaneers' assault upon the city. Nevertheless, we did not remain within the nave, but made our way up several flights of stone stairs which led us to a gallery running round the body of the cathedral, called, as my father said, the "clerestory." Through one of the windows overlooking this gallery we were able to watch some of the struggle taking place in the city.

Although too high above the ground to be able to distinguish between buccaneers and Spaniard, we could tell how the fight was progressing. The main street of the city led straight from the gate we had helped to barricade up to the cathedral, so that from our windows we were able to obtain almost an uninterrupted view.

"Tell me how matters are going, Arthur," begged my father, whose exhaustion forced him to lie stretched out upon the ground. I had been kneeling by him at first, as in duty bound, but must confess I longed to be with Big Dixon and the others at the windows, watching the attack upon Panama. At my father's request, then, I joyfully sprang to my feet, and climbed into a niche from which I could observe much that was going on.

"They haven't forced the gates yet," I cried. "There, one of the demi-cannon has again been fired. But look! There's quite a lot of confusion near the gate. Some of the buccaneers must have forced their way in!"

"The musket-fire has stopped," commented Dixon. "They're evidently fighting hand-to-hand at the gate."

"They're falling back, father. Yes, they're turning to run."

"Who? The Spaniards?"

"Yes. Ah! Now they've disappeared from view. They've manned one of the trenches, I expect. Yes, musket-fire has broken out again from each side."

And so we watched the taking of Panama. Between the cathedral and the gate the streets were almost deserted, save where an occasional brave woman stood at the door of her house, wondering how events were moving. For a long time all the fighting—and it must have been fierce, for the defence was stubborn—took place in the vicinity of the gate. There we saw the buccaneers swing the demi-cannon around until they faced inwards upon the city, and discharge them upon the Spaniards.

Palabra it was, I later heard, who was chiefly responsible for forcing the main gate. As though bearing a life charmed alike against bullet and blade, he had charged with waving hanger at the gunners serving the demi-cannon, and cut down three within as many minutes. Greatly heartened by his example, and remembering the vast treasure

Panama was reputed to hold, on swept the other buccaneers in his wake, to capture the demi-cannon and use them, as I have related, against their previous owners.

But if the buccaneers were courageous because of the treasure they hoped to win, the Spaniards were no less so, knowing what fate they might expect if Panama should fall. Between the main gate and the cathedral numerous trenches had been dug, and near most of them were more guns, laid so as to command the streets along which the buccaneers would approach. Each of these barricades were stubbornly defended, and when one had been taken and the buccaneers were advancing against the next, from every house that flanked the street along which they came, Spaniards poured upon them a heavy fire. The losses on both sides were frightful, but though the buccaneers were attacking, and so were the more exposed, the Spaniards lost far more men, for every time a barricade was overrun, all Spaniards unable to retreat were ruthlessly cut down. Morgan had given the order, "No quarter!" and never was order more rigorously obeyed.

Perhaps it took two hours for the defenders to be driven back to their last barricade, which was full in sight of the cathedral, being scarcely one hundred yards away. The exact time I cannot say, for when one's interest is gripped so intensely as was mine, all thought of the flying minutes is forgotten. I saw the surviving Dons fall back upon the last refuge with mixed feelings. I could not help admiring them for the tremendous defence they were making. I felt sorry as I realised how many of them, ay, women and children as well as men, were likely to fall victims to the cruelty of the buccaneers; and all the time I knew that success for Morgan's men meant safety for our party.

There came a lull in the fighting before the buccaneers began their final assault. Doubtless there were many sharp-shooters in houses already passed who had to be dealt with. While they waited for their enemies, I could see the Dons working feverishly to improve their defences, and presently a Spanish priest could be seen blessing the defenders, standing in full view as he lifted his hands in benediction, while the Spaniards knelt bareheaded before him.

A single musket-shot suddenly broke the short silence of the mutual truce. For a moment I thought it was but a shot fired at random, for the grey-haired priest remained in his attitude of benediction. But presently he swayed slightly upon his feet, before pitching forward into the trench lined by his countrymen.

As though the priest's death had been a prearranged signal for attack, the buccaneers came swarming along the street, still shouting lustily, although many of their voices were hoarse from the cries they had uttered during the long day's fighting. But the Spaniards did not wait under cover, firing at the buccaneers, as one would have expected. As though infuriated beyond endurance at the cruel shot which had robbed them of their priest, they waited only long enough to fire one well-directed volley that brought down many of their assailants and caused a momentary stoppage of the rest. Then out from cover swarmed the Dons, some with sword or cutlass in hand, others with clubbed musket, and with yells every whit as fierce as those of the buccaneers, they swept down the street to grapple with their foes.

It was magnificent madness. As though for the moment bereft of fear, the Dons flung themselves recklessly upon their hated foes. Weapons rose and fell; opponents died in each other's arms; all nice rules of fair fighting were forgotten in that wild tussle between battle-maddened men. By their impetuous charge the Spaniards had forfeited all the advantages of their barricade. The Dons who lined the houses upon either side of the street were no longer able to fire upon the buccaneers for fear of hurting their own comrades. Hand-to-hand fighting was the salt of life to many of the bold followers of Morgan. The Spaniards had given away all their advantages because of their wild anger at the death of their priest.

Yet for all that it looked as though the fury of the Spaniards would quench the recklessness of the buccaneers. At first nothing could be seen as to how the participants of that wild mêlée were faring. Then Fiddler Jim gave an exclamation of dismay. "The Brethren are retreating!" he cried.

It was true. Back they fell for about twenty yards. For some reason or other the Spaniards did not follow. Maybe they feared a trap, maybe they were exhausted by their furious effort. Whatever the reason, they neither followed up their success nor fell back to the shelter of their trenches. Instead they stood in scattered knots of men amongst the heaps of slain, "like sheep waiting for the butchers," as Dixon put it, who, for all his hatred of the Spaniards, could not help feeling pity for them now.

I saw Morgan appear in front of his men, and guessed the nature of his harangue. How he would curse them, with that deep-throated voice of his! How his dark eyes would sweep them with scornful gaze, making them feel ashamed of their retreat! How he would remind them, with bitter, scathing words, that he had not brought them to Panama to see them run away! Well Morgan knew how to stir up the passions of the reckless men he commanded!

Presently he turned again towards the foe, and flourished his weapon over his head before commencing to run, a lone figure, against the Dons. For a moment I held my breath in suspense. Were the buccaneers going to allow their Admiral to charge alone, and find death upon the weapons of the Spaniards? My fears were not long retained. With a united shout, louder than any I had heard that day, the Brethren rushed behind their valiant leader.

That was virtually the end of the fight. For a few moments the Dons resisted; then most of those still living broke and fled. Some few knots still fought desperately, but not for long. Ruthlessly the fighters were cut down, and when presently the buccaneers split up in tiny parties to hunt out and slay any surviving Spaniards, not a Don remained alive in the street.

"Panama is taken!" I cried to my father, and then the effects of the many excitements of that day combined to unman me. I put out my hand to clutch the gallery rail to steady myself, missed, tottered blindly for a minute, then pitched forward in a dead faint.

I came to myself again wondering where I could be. I would have asked, but a warning hand was placed over my mouth, and Big Dixon's voice whispered in my ear, "Steady, boy; Knocker is down below in the nave, and so far as I can tell he's up to no good."

Memory flooded back upon me, and I recalled the plottings against Morgan that I had heard during the march across the Isthmus. Forgetting the weakness which had caused me to faint, I struggled to my knees and peered through the opening in the gallery rail. Down below some score of the buccaneers were foraging hither and thither, and amongst them I recognised Palabra, Diaz, and many others of Knocker's fellow-plotters.

"What are they after?" I whispered to Big Dixon.

"The treasure of the cathedral, I expect," he returned cautiously. "Doubtless they have questioned some prisoner, and hope to put the hoard in a secret place for their own use."

"Shall we let them know we're here?" I asked.

"No," advised Big Dixon. "If they're up to no good, they'd be as likely to kill us as not if they discovered us."

But in spite of our caution our presence was revealed to them, for one of the prowling buccaneers came upon us where we lay, and before we could silence him had dashed down to the others with the news. Knocker rallied his men, and we could see them drawing their weapons.

Big Dixon attempted to prevent friction by showing himself above the gallery rails.

"Hello, comrades!" he cried. "No need for alarm. There are only friends here."

"Friends?" sneered Knocker. "Spies, more likely. I bet Morgan's pup is with you."

"If you mean young Ellis, yes! But he's no more spy than I am. What is there to spy upon?"

For answer, Knocker suddenly aimed a pistol at him, and had not Big Dixon hurriedly stumbled backwards, he might have been killed, for the bullet smacked viciously against the wall behind, in line with the spot where my comrade had been standing.

"Quick, lads," urged Big Dixon. "Get under the best cover you can. There's nothing for it but to fight. Knocker and his men will give no mercy."

As I knelt behind a protecting corner, musket nuzzled against my cheek, I could not help reflecting bitterly how cruel Fate could be. Now that the danger of death or capture by the Spaniards was over, we were likely to be slain by men from the ranks of those we had looked upon as our allies.

Yet there was scant time for bitterness. There came the clattering of feet along the gallery, and the buccaneers came into sight, firing as they approached. Their musket-balls whistled uncomfortably close, in spite of our partial shelter, but, nevertheless, we returned their fire, dropping two men at our first volley. My own shot, directed at the villainous Knocker himself, was quite ineffective, much to my chagrin.

And then Big Dixon did a stupendously foolish thing, albeit it was probably the saving of us all. Leaving his shelter, he suddenly dashed full tilt towards the buccaneers. A pistol cracked, but failed to check his progress. The stalwart Palabra barred his way, with bloodstained hanger raised. Crack! Dixon's fist, lashing upwards, tumbled the fellow over on to his back. Next moment Big Dixon had clutched hold of Knocker, and the two were twisting and writhing in a fierce conflict.

Though in size Knocker could not compare with my gigantic comrade, he was, nevertheless, no mean fighter. As though by common consent both the buccaneers and ourselves left these two combatants alone, and watched tensely the issue of the duel.

Although Big Dixon had Knocker's left arm pinned tightly against his side, the buccaneer captain had his right arm free, and quickly managed to draw a dagger from his belt. As he plunged it towards Big Dixon's side, I closed my eyes so as to escape seeing my comrade's fall. A gasp of joy from Fiddler Jim made me open them again. Knocker's blow had never fallen. In the nick of time Big Dixon had seized the man's wrist, and wrested the knife from him.

And now, for one brief instant, Big Dixon released his hold upon the buccaneer. With a swift movement he stooped, and seized Knocker by the waist. Then high in the air, right over his head, he lifted the shrieking man, and advanced quickly to the gallery rail.

"Here ends Knocker!" he cried in a loud voice, and braced himself to fling the buccaneer down to the stone floor below.

A sudden blare of bugles from the plaza outside, followed immediately by a clangour below, stayed him in the nick of time. He remained with the buccaneer still poised above his head while the rest of us looked towards the door of the cathedral.

Just inside, followed by many of his most trusted men, heavily armed, stood Admiral Morgan.

As though carven in stone, Knocker's fellow-conspirators watched whilst Morgan crossed to the stairs leading to the gallery, and slowly mounted them. Close behind came Captain Gentle, and other loyal buccaneers. As the Admiral approached, Big Dixon lowered the man he had been prepared to cast to his death, but still kept a watch upon him to guard against treachery.

"Captain Knocker," said Morgan sternly, as he confronted the discomfited buccaneer, "the city of Panama has been set fire to in a dozen places. One of the Brethren caught doing this has confessed that you gave orders for the city to be burnt. What have you to say?"

The buccaneer's downcast eyes and white face were sufficient signs of his guilt, even though he made no reply.

"Captain Knocker," went on the Admiral, "you were given orders to proceed at once to the harbour, and seize any vessels lying there. Instead, I find you fighting comrades of mine in this cathedral where, I believe, you have come in search of private loot. What have you to say?"

Again there was no reply. Morgan gave a sign to Captain Gentle, who stepped forward.

"Captain Knocker, and you, Palabra and Diaz, I place you under arrest, on a charge of conspiring against our Admiral, and plotting to steal for yourselves treasure that ought to be shared by all the Brethren of the expedition. Follow me!"

In silence the three chief conspirators did as they were commanded. The loyal buccaneers took their weapons from them before they went, and they passed out of the cathedral expecting nothing less than death as a punishment for their treachery. Admiral Morgan then turned upon the rest of the traitors, and after a few fiery words that made them look as though they would like the ground to open up and swallow them, he sent them back to their duty. And then he turned towards us.

"Well, Sir Hugh!" he said, grasping my father's wasted hand in his own powerful one. "Who would have thought we should have met here, of all places, after so many years. You see, Arthur, the old witch of Port Royal was not far out in what she promised. 'You'll be led by a villain,' said she. Well, Diaz was villain enough, you'll allow. 'You'll walk beside the son of an old friend.' Didn't you and I journey together most of the way? 'You'll be deceived by the men you trust most.' Well, that was Knocker, whom, I must confess, I was mad enough to trust. So she prophesied aright, as you see."

"Yes, sir," I agreed, "but she forgot to add one thing; that you'd meet the old friend whose son journeyed with you on the expedition. Thank Heaven, that though she didn't prophesy it, nevertheless it came true."

"Amen," murmured Morgan, and I was surprised to see tears in his eyes.